Errors
of Evaluation

Paola Pica

Clink
Street

London | New York

Published by Clink Street Publishing 2016

Copyright © 2016

First edition.

ISBN:
978-1-911110-32-3 paperback
978-1-911110-33-0 ebook

*For my translator Janice and for all translators,
because their skill makes our books enjoyable
for everyone, everywhere.*

Chapter One
Marco's Error of Evaluation

I loathed her from practically the first moment I laid eyes on her. Because I am a weaver of spells and she would never have been trapped in my web. I felt that. I knew it to be true.

Francesca introduced her to me one winter's day, after 'officially' informing me that her cousin would drop in on us one morning for coffee.

Rather surprising this, it being the first time that Francesca had ever received a visitor at home.

She told me that her cousin had turned up again last night out of the blue, phoning her after never having been seen or heard from in the last ten years.

Now, Francesca didn't know that there was no need to announce this. I said 'officially' before, because I had listened in on their entire conversation over one of the several handsets that I had had installed throughout the house.

I won't dwell on what I remember about that phone call, because it is still all too painful.

It was the warmth of Francesca's farewell to her cousin, coming after a decidedly cool beginning of the conversation, that provoked in me a pang of wild jealousy.

Well known for her icy tone was my current lady, so her voice pierced my ear like a stiletto. It meant that despite all my hard work, perhaps it was still possible for someone to make something vibrate within her —— something new and not meant for me alone.

Now, what could that woman want, coming from God-knows-what shared past, of which I knew nothing?

My women have always been mine alone and they have to appear to be cold and unavailable to anyone else, male or female, because emotions bring people together, and there is always the danger that a little warmth can reawaken hidden desires for joining and sharing.

That night I dreamt that Francesca forded a freezing mountain stream — she who cannot stand the cold and even at home is always bundled up from head to toe.

Well, I know that there are also other reasons why she never uncovers herself, not even in the summer, but I don't want to get into talking about how she somatises her coldness to distance herself from others.

At least, that's what she used to be like. Now ... I'm not so sure. No, she can't have changed.

As I was saying about my dream: she was crossing that icy torrent, legs and trousers wet up to the groin, trying to reach someone there on the other side.

But I couldn't see the face of the person waiting for her. He or she was half-hidden by a great rock and from there, patting it invitingly with a hand that I could see, the person was saying, "Come on, feel how warm and sunny it is here".

And Francesca kept trying and laughing. Laughing! She who may only laugh with me; she who I had molded to never smile at anyone without first giving me a quick glance to seek my approval.

She knows perfectly well that I want her to be gelid and distant with others. She is to respond only to me, because she must be mine and mine alone.

I awoke in a cold sweat, convinced that I was still there in that stream where I had thrown myself in after her to stop her.

Whatever ... a dream like any other, really.

When Francesca announced her cousin's visit, I was all innocence. I even said that it was about time that I met someone from her past because I wanted to know everything about her.

2

Every time that I came out with one of these things, her eyes would light up and she misinterpreted my sense of possessiveness for something else — perhaps as love. But really it was only ever about ownership, and so that I could dispel my suspicions about her. Because I knew full well how easy it had been to take her.

I had wanted her so much and I had to have her no matter what — just as I have always seized anything I really wanted — but love is something else entirely. It's that thing over which almost all of my patients come crying to me about … and obviously I let them weep and I console them and I even give them advice because that's my job and, in theory, I know all about feelings.

As for me, only Beauty exists, so when I see it, I grab it without getting into any of those contorted justifications conferred on it by so-called aesthetes, who even go so far as to drag philosophy into it all in order to justify their needs. And they come here to tell me how Beauty (necessarily with a capital 'B') equals Good (capital 'G' as before), etcetera, etcetera, etcetera.

Francesca's ex-husband was one of those. I ask you: how could she have put up with him for twenty years? How boring conversation with him was …. Still, if I wanted her, that was the road I would have to take.

As I was saying about beauty, about what is beautiful for me — when I want something, I never concern myself with who it belongs to or who might have more right to it than me.

And Francesca is very very beautiful.

Anyway, at eleven o'clock in the morning, I heard the doorbell ring while I was in the bathroom. I had gone in just a few minutes beforehand because I did not want to be present when they met, seeing each other again after so long and especially after some event of which I had been unaware. Even though I was very curious about it all, I did not want this to show. It made me angry that she was part of Francesca's past — a past that I thought I had completely fathomed. Evidently, this was not the case.

Here was a new detail popping up, something that Francesca had kept back from me, just when I had felt certain that I had filtered out not just her thoughts but also her capacity to produce any.

I always do this to my women: break them down, that is. She was like a diamond ring on my finger — meant to be shown off. Flaunted about, like my cars. Always very valuable, but above all flashy.

I was dying of curiosity, given that within a few minutes and before my very eyes, Elena would be the first person to have emerged from Francesca's past (besides her family, that is, and her ex-husband, who I had known and robbed).

Curiosity to the nth degree, nothing more than that. Because hatred took over from the moment we shook hands. A ferocious odium which I immediately recognized as stemming from having to admit my inability to ever subjugate her.

Her handshake had that positive energy which is unmistakeable and so rare.

As soon as I had heard the entry-phone, I had slipped into the bathroom. For another reason as well — my uncontainable love of theatrics which I have always used to cloak my life. I wanted to impress, arriving as if by chance, while the two women were busy in who-knows-what kind of conversation after so many years, but having shared all of a life up until that moment of rupture, of trauma, of mystery.

I would eavesdrop a bit before coming into the kitchen, where I knew that Francesca would entertain her rather special guest.

She loved the kitchen in my house at least as much as I did. Indeed, beyond the fact that it is comfortable and welcoming, Francesca knew that I am at heart a man who loves his slippers and his hearth.

Yes, I have lived almost all of my life burrowed within the various houses where I have dwelled — that is to say, made my dens — and where I have drawn in my partners, forcing them to live an extremely closeted life. A life in which they must take care of me alone, and must share those rhythms I keep, as of a rat always in hiding. Naturally all this still allowed for the daily exception of the hours of work for me and for them. As for myself (distinct from rats, which at least come out at night), I also work from home, so I can go for weeks without having to leave the house.

It was perfect with Francesca because she didn't work; had never worked, she hadn't. So she was completely at my disposal — at my service, you might say. To the point that I've often asked myself how the hell she spent the hours when I was in therapy, since she never went out anymore without me. It's true that she devoured my books, with that typical thirst for knowledge that comes from emulating someone in order to rise to their level.

The kitchen is the part of my house that I have always preferred because that is where tending to me is revealed through the different senses. The sense of taste, first of all, but also the sense of smell and of sight, all of which I have always wanted to have completely satiated at meal times.

And Francesca was simply a Queen in the kitchen. An excellent cook (like all my other women), but she took especial care in setting the table — in a slightly eccentric way, I'll admit, but truly exceptional nonetheless.

That morning I had seen her get out her weird demitasse cups and arrange them on one of those cloths of hers which are not really table linen but, even if they are of absolutely no use whatsoever, they bring to mind the creation of a famous designer.

To dazzle — I never had to teach her how to do that, nor was I jealous, because every time (which is to say, always) she amazed someone, the compliment inevitably fell to me, who owned such a Treasure.

Everyone envied me about her, because she certainly never passed unobserved in anything she did.

As far as that goes, her Pygmalion had been her husband, who had chosen her because she was very beautiful, very much younger than him (by now we are both over 60), inexperienced and not at all sure of herself, in spite of her physical appearance.

He, too, had molded her not a little according to his own image and likeness, the same way he had always — ever since he was a student — aimed to influence situations, destabilizing individuals and group equilibrium, in order to always direct everyone's attention onto himself and onto his own "brilliant" ideas. And what was always shining brilliantly was his fortune, which, with very little effort on his part, distinguished him from the other penniless students.

In short, by dint of repeating to her how beautiful she was, and how whatever she put on looked better on her than on any other woman on the face of the Earth, including fashion models, he had convinced her. Even convinced her that she had the right to be daring in all aspects of their life together, not least of all in interior decorating.

When I plucked her up, Francesca had already achieved a level of self-confidence about her own worth and about her own sense of aesthetics, so that she relied completely on her looks, which, according to her, must shine down upon all that surrounded her.

I have never been jealous of her with that man, since, anyway, I was the one who stole his Gem.

Getting back to Elena's visit — the cousin re-found — it was imperative for me to make one of my solemn on-stage appearances, in which my lack of formality, together with my unusual looks, always manages to win everyone's favor. Well, yes, because I don't think that I pass unobserved either, with my head completely shaved and my penetrating eyes, above a nose which I wouldn't call Grecian or aquiline, but simply significant.

I dress casually, having chosen to live at ease and ignore formality, that is, without caring about what anyone else thinks.

And I do like to make an impression.

To make sure, I always let it be known that I'm a shrink, a fact which never fails to fascinate and induce awe in others.

I had heard Francesca tell Elena over the phone that I am a psychiatrist, so half the battle was already won. I could saunter into the kitchen as though by chance, even though Francesca had told me about the impending visit and had added, "I can't wait to introduce you to Elena. You are completely different from Massimo and I can just imagine her face."

Instead, when I entered the scene, there was neither surprise nor awe in those green eyes. Only a mixture of good manners, expressed in the way she held out her hand, and of the cordiality, with which she welcomed the presence of a new person in her cousin's life.

I said so before; I hated her immediately.

She was perfectly at ease and interested in getting to know me, as she would have been even had I had been a banker or any other kind of doctor — something more banal, I mean.

I quickly realized that she was immune to that effect which shrinks induce in everyone. Immune, that is, to that niggling feeling which makes you feel analyzed by a penetrating and expert gaze (in the true sense of the word) — by our piercing look which is able to bare the soul.

Nothing of that sort in Elena. And it was made clear to me from that very first moment, as I felt her strong honest handshake and peered into those eyes which, (damn them) penetrated into my own soul instead.

I know only too well that when you come across this type (in group therapy, for example), they can bring tumbling down the whole castle which you have built around yourself. And which you had believed to be strong, because you had bent others to your will as you liked and according to your own image.

As things stood, a serpent was insinuating itself into my private life. I was enough of an expert to know that the venom which it could inject might be a soothing antidote to my own poison. And it was all there in those emerald eyes, as pure as diamonds.

As I just said, someone like that truly shakes the walls

which have taken years of painstaking mastery to raise. But my castle is built with playing cards. I had always played cards, or rather, I should say, that I had always cheated at cards — since my university days, since my family crowed over my degree, since going abroad to America for my doctorate and residency, throughout my whole career.

I've never stopped cheating at cards. But no one knows that.

Above all, I have cheated and do cheat on my patients and on my partners, who I encounter on different levels of course, although the two levels do sometimes overlap, due to some questionable counter-transference on my part.

It's so easy for me to enchant them, manipulating their minds and their hearts with an ability I seem to have always been blessed with. I have to admit that on this point my professionalism is debatable, but it is also equally true that my intuition and insight have always been the One True Pearl of my life as a mystifier.

I did not want this intruder to undermine the effects of a talent so rare, nor did I want her to deaden my magic power.

That this would all happen if I were not ready to neutralize her, I understood as I shook her hand and looked her in the face. I found myself having to tear my eyes away from hers — me, who never looks away from anyone, man or woman, until they do so first. That is how I am with patients, friends, acquaintances, or even strangers. Because a penetrating gaze touches the essence of the ego in front of you, which almost always feels naked, either because it really is denuded, or because it is only threatened with exposure from the supposed power of the eyes of a Master, which is instead often only impudence and deceit.

She seemed so calm (even if a little excited to find her cousin again) and so completely interested in the simple fact that Francesca and I were together, that she did not refer to my profession at all. She quickly switched to using my first name, even though, at the outset, she had used my title and had been immediately corrected by Francesca.

Not even a vague attempt at a "Pleased to meet you, Doctor," which is something that I had expected.

I've already mentioned how I immediately read from her handshake and from her eyes that it would be impossible for me to manage a transference in her. I realized that it would be impossible were I even to spend time working at it.

I had to neutralize her, until — as soon as possible — I could get her out of the way. But it had to be done without raising any suspicion in the eyes of Francesca.

That decision of mine became an obsession for me for months — I'd say even for a couple of years — and even though we immediately began to meet up, I worked steadily during that time to make sure that we mixed less and less.

The two of them were very happy to have found each other again and Francesca surprised me with how willing she was to jump back into an old relationship with family and with a friend.

We had, by now, been together for two years. Her desire at the beginning to keep up a social life and to go out shopping had by now practically ceased. That had taken me quite a lot of effort.

Yet I heard them planning to hit the outlets together and to drop by 'that open-air market' where they used to go ten years ago, just to see if it was still there and to see if the clothes there were still as unique as before.

But they were only talking about this just before Elena left.

For two hours before that, they had done nothing else except catch up with each other about their lives, given that the gap to fill was not just a few days or a few months. Yet there was not even a hint about their breakup.

I immediately noticed that Elena was giving way quite a lot to an unusually loquacious Francesca, who was happy to show me off. She demonstrated a sincere interest in this new (as she quickly defined it) 'world' of Francesca's.

That term gave me a good deal of food for thought, because it lightly but precisely defined Francesca's new existential situation. With that word, Elena had demonstrated that she perceived a total change in her cousin — in her daily life, first of all, but also in her way of dealing with it.

As far as I could understand, they had dropped each other at a time when Francesca had become mired in a boring swamp (painless and problem-free though it was), alongside a man in a perennial state of dissatisfaction, which had proved contagious.

I also knew that, together with him, Francesca had followed her dreams of studying at university, collecting art, sailing and attending splendid social events, but that both of them had always halted after the first few enthusiastic attendances, because their limited ability to persevere made their goals unreachable. I heard Francesca place most of the blame on Massimo and I heard Elena rush to share that opinion, but I don't know if she was convinced.

In fact, Francesca and Elena seemed to me to be completely different from each other, and it was immediately evident that Elena was blessed with a decisive and tenacious personality.

She was the complete opposite of Francesca, whom I had netted back then like a butterfly. When we two couples used to go out together, she had been flitting from one thing that caught her interest to another, concentrating on that thing for a few months, spending money on the equipment necessary for whatever it required, always buying the best and most expensive brands.

All that, only to consign it a short time later to some corner or other of the large house in which she lived with her husband, and almost always to that enormous room which she had designated as her own study. To study what, or to work on what, I have always had a hard time understanding.

One of the first pieces of 'necessary and indispensable' equipment that ended up there was a magnificent drawing table, suitable for the busy work schedule of a talented architect of some renown. She had immediately felt an absolute need for it as soon as she had she signed up for classes in architecture after some ten years of marriage.

I have to say that I was quite impressed with that table, placed like a throne before a large window. The window gave onto the sloping front lawn, and a view which followed the horizon as far as the eye could see, down the hill to their riding stables. At that time riding was Massimo's main occupation. Unfortunately, managing such a large establishment was more difficult for him than taking his long rides on horseback — something which had intrigued Francesca and not just her alone.

When I first met her, Francesca had already dropped out of university after the first year (during which she had sat not a single exam) — amazed at how boring the classes were.

There had been the same flame of enthusiasm for collaborating with her fashion-designer friend on creating new outfits, and with an artist–artisan that they knew who was well-known in the field of wrought iron.

Then she got interested in trite New Age psycho-babble, taking up lightweight popularized pseudo-psychology before latching onto the serious Psychology (with a capital 'P'), which she was doing when we met and she had become my patient.

During that same time, we also saw each other outside my practice with our respective partners — her husband and my then companion, who was also an ex-patient of mine.

Our foursome lasted for about a year, but I had got her into my head from the first moment that I had seen her at a dinner at the house of friends.

She had come in, her husband a few steps behind her, just when we were about to sit down to dinner. I can see her now as though it were yesterday: a very elegant young lady who could even have presented herself dressed in a monk's habit, since her beauty would have eclipsed everything else. I remember a blue light striking me, because she was dressed in that color, which heightened her pale skin and her blonde shoulder-length hair, styled like Greta Garbo's, if you know what I mean.

I know perfectly well that it was at that moment that I decided to appropriate that jewel for myself. But I also knew that I would have to move with prudence — the sort of prudence I usually deployed in these cases.

I have never started a new relationship by concerning myself to first clear the boards of the current one. I mean to say that I have never broken up with anyone without having first ensured that I had a ready substitute. Therefore, I never started up with a new one if it meant that there was any risk of finding myself without the old one still at home.

It's just one way of keeping the home fires always smouldering (even if not crackling) during the changeover, because as I've already said, I do like my home and hearth more than most men.

In fact, only once I've started a physical rapport in a new affair do I break off all relations with my actual official companion, who then finds herself completely baffled by my total lack of desire for her. At the bottom of my heart, I'm a true monogamist.

Apart from everything else, this tactic of mine provokes perplexity to turn into rage once all is revealed and then my task is easier, because pride leads her to bundle her belongings together and stomp out. Easy as pie. This is what is meant by poking people in their weak spots to your own advantage. But to do so, you need a deep understanding of what motivates the human soul.

Fortunately, however, Francesca had no pride ... nor even dignity.

Therefore, there was no danger of the house being temporarily left cold while I was ensuring that the other candidate for my bed was the right one. She pretended to not notice anything, and I think that she indulged in one of her little fantasies in which she was absolutely indispensable to her hot-spirited knight, who was now flagging a bit from age.

Besides, she wouldn't have known where to go. Unlike the others, all of whom had owned houses, or at least had jobs with which to support themselves.

But I made an error in my evaluation, and Elena had

contributed greatly to speed up the timing of her departure. The result: that time there was an empty period — an 'interregnum' — at my hearth.

Getting back to Elena's visit on that winter's morning at the beginning of my third year living with her cousin, Francesca was happy that Elena declared that she had found herself in front of a completely different Francesca, more decisive and serene, more convinced (these were her very words) about her new choice of life. With this judgement, she demonstrated immediately her undoubted talent for perception and sensitivity, even if she could not yet imagine how much effort I had dedicated to manipulating Francesca over the last two years.

But I knew already that she would get there, and it wouldn't even take long before she did, given that acumen which I perceived in her and which was slyly agitating me.

Because when it came to understanding the Conscious and the Unconscious, it was me and me alone who should have been the Expert. So much so that, all things considered, I thought that it should have been viewed in a positive light that I had brought her to achieve stability, when she went from being a butterfly to a rat like me. Even Elena said that she appeared to be happy, didn't she? She was happy.

This Francesca, who was brand-new for Elena, carried out beautifully the duties of the perfect hostess with coffee and chocolates (she's crazy about chocolates), and for a while I steered a middle course through the conversation. But it was so totally banal; not a single allusion to the break-up of ten years ago. Perhaps they would never talk about it in front of me, I thought. I hastily put together a plan — deciding that it would be even better to use my propensity for eavesdropping from just outside the kitchen door, after first excusing myself to attend to an urgent telephone call.

This was already a tried and true method — I just had to flatten myself against the wall and make sure that the small light on the sideboard in the entrance hall didn't project my shadow onto the floor.

In fact, the lamp was turned on, given that it was a particularly gloomy winter's morning — nearly dark.

The two of them stayed there, sitting at the table, nibbling the assortment of chocolates, which Francesca had arranged in 'her' Liberty glassware, which had once belonged to Massimo's grandmother.

Before I left, she asked me if I wanted another cup of coffee from the pot she was brewing and, when I declined, she pouted like a kitten and kissed me on a spot somewhere between my mouth and my cheek as I moved away, while I said that I needed to dash off to the telephone.

I managed to position myself in such a way as to clearly hear their voices.

"Come on now, tell me right away how you feel about this new situation and if you are really happy."

"I am, truly I am. I feel different. Don't you think I've changed?"

"The only thing I can see is that you are thinner than ever. I'd say maybe even a little too thin. But as beautiful as always and your eyes … they shine more than I have ever seen them shine before. You look as though you are in Seventh Heaven. Certainly not like I saw them the last time — on the boat — when I don't know what came over you. I've asked myself over the years what it was all about."

"Now, now … stop right there. I don't want to talk about it. Anyway, yes, I am in Seventh Heaven. With Marco I have found everything that I was searching for in life. I love him and he feels the same about me, believe me. We couldn't be better."

I was angrily reflecting on the fact that Elena was also diplomatic, since she respected Francesca's wishes and did not insist on the story about the boat, when she suddenly said: "Just a minute, I want to fetch the paper napkins from the dresser in the entrance hall. It's just outside…"

I hurriedly disappeared into the room next door to the kitchen, and thank goodness the day was so horrible that no one could stay on the terrace between the two rooms.

Elena left about half an hour later, and Francesca came looking for me downstairs, where I was sitting on the sofa of the parlour-cum-study.

She found me absorbed in reading one of my books. My books … she devoured them, memorized a few tracts, and then pathetically played them back to me during our private conversations. She especially did this during our group-therapy sessions.

I let her get away with it because that was only another tile in the larger mosaic of dominance I was creating; the process of identification is slow and it takes patience as well as time. It's like the growing of a fetus from which a new person must develop, made in the image and likeness of the stronger of the two. It's not just about behaviors and the mental 'posturings' which are rationally imposed from Without. It must be for the weakest to choose, and to believe that he is choosing — to own the process — in his desperate need to look like the other, that is, like the model with which he has slowly but surely identified himself.

And on this point, I have always considered that it is enough to know a person's weaknesses to be able to do what you want with him. For Francesca (who already recognized perfectly well her own her physical gifts), her weak point was the violent need to prove to herself that her failure in her studies and her pretension of having a profession without a degree were not at all important when it came to a quick mind such as hers, that is, such as mine.

But, while I assiduously carried out this undercover activity, I made a mistake. A fatal error in reading the situation. And one in which Elena would have had a determining role.

A couple of months later, during dinner at Elena's house, where Francesca had dragged me against my will (in things that don't really matter, I've always let her believe that she was the strong one in our relationship — a bit like giving candy to a child to keep it quiet), I let that exact phrase slip out, that is, that it's enough to know a person's weak points to do what you want with him.

No professional in my field should ever state such a thing, much less should I have done so in those circumstances.

Notwithstanding my intuition about Elena's ability to sense things, I had never noticed her sensitivity, that is, her ability to perceive the most secret intentions of the person in front of her.

Francesca had gone to the toilet and we were still gathered around the table with another two of Elena's friends who Francesca had often heard mentioned in their 'previous' life.

I remember that bit of thoughtlessness as being a false step that I should never have taken and of which, at that moment, I did not realize the gravity. How could I have been so foolish as to pronounce that sentence while addressing Elena? After I had never spoken a word to her, not even to compliment her on her cooking.

After such recklessness on my part, evidently due to me involuntarily lowering my guard for some reason which I cannot explain, I said goodbye forever to any success with what had been my strategy for getting rid of her, to keep her from delving any deeper into the relationship between me and Francesca.

I've had plenty of practice with this method of distancing the enemy and I continue to use it every time I find disagreeable the company of a new acquaintance. Obviously it is different with patients; I manage to put up with them because they pay me, even though I could strangle some of them.

By my acting in this way with people, the person in question, as he does not feel accepted, enters into a state of insecurity which does not allow him to move forward, or it may even cause him to withdraw, if our acquaintance is more than nodding.

This is how I have always managed to isolate my life as a couple from the rest of the world.

That Sunday lunch, I always spoke to the other two guests and to Francesca, even when expressing my opinion about Elena's statements.

I have to say that she led me a merry dance, because, as if she had intuited my intention, she played a subtle game, with nary a reproachful look in my direction, even though you would expect that from someone who has found an absolute boor at her table.

When Francesca begged pardon for having to leave the interesting conversation for a moment, the lady in the other couple had been talking about how her thirty-something-year-old daughter had shown herself to be vulnerable in all of her love stories and how she always came out of them in a bad state. Her husband had chimed in, adding that even that blockhead she had brought home as her last boyfriend had managed to make her suffer.

Before absenting herself, Francesca had expressed her opinion that people tend to repeat the same mistakes in each union, without ever having learned very much from their previous relationships. Unless, she added with a warm glance towards me, one does not have the good fortune to find at a certain point someone 'completely compatible' (here remarked with an intense tone) who finally induces one to not do it again.

This is how a short debate arose on how to interpret 'compatible'. Did it mean 'complementary'? Or perhaps the term simply alluded to the capacity of one of the two of them to accept the other one totally, so as not to lose him or her.

"No", said Elena heatedly, "that behavior would be unhealthy; it would even be masochistic."

It was at that point that Francesca had to dash to the bathroom, to check in the mirror if a fishbone had damaged her gums. It was nothing serious, so no one made a fuss about it and the conversation continued.

It was just at that point, when I was about to express my opinion (being the expert in the matter and perhaps because Francesca was not present), that, without mitigating my words, I turned to Elena and said, "Compatibility within a couple does not exist, because individuals mutate according to the situation and the only reason for which some couples seem

17

to function is because one of the two has the pure and simple capacity to identify the weak points of the other and exploits them to his own advantage."

It took only a fraction of a second. I recognized the harshness of my assertion, and I corrected it by adding: "I meant to the advantage of the couple … of course". But it was too late, because the tone which I had used was not the neutral voice of a professional who is expounding on a theory and criticizes it negatively, given that he is not treating a patient. Instead, I had spoken fervently as though I had been talking about myself.

The other two did not seem to have noticed anything in particular, but Elena's antennas picked it up. Unusually for me, who is always on guard, I was sure then and there that I had remedied the erroneous evaluation of the person I had in front of me.

It would take me about two years before I realized that Elena had found me out that day — all about the dirty game I was playing with Francesca's mind. I would discover this when spying on one of their phone conversations at the end — so painful and so totally disadvantageous for Francesca — of my affair with her.

Chapter Two
Massimo's Error of Evaluation

I turned sixty not long ago and I am paying for the biggest mistake of my life, made more than thirty years ago and which I tried to fix by taking my own life — this absurd life that does not belong to me, which is no longer the golden existence into which I was born and raised.

I am in a hospital bed in the private clinic where my brother wanted me placed, he himself shouldering all the expenses. I wouldn't have been able to oppose this even had I wanted to, because I was unconscious and in grave danger of dying, having shot myself in the heart with a .22 caliber gun. Or, at least, that's what I thought I had done.

Two wrongs do not make a right: you can't fix one mistake by making another even bigger one. I shouldn't have missed the target.

I spend too much time thinking, now that they sedate me less after bringing me out of my medically-induced coma.

It's probably the drugs, but my life has been passing before my eyes, this life of infamy.

It's strange: when I realized that I was thinking as a person awake and that I was not dreaming, much less living 'elsewhere', after the dreaded tunnel, the first thought I had was that I should hide the gun with which I had hurt myself, convinced that it was next to me on the living-room floor of my house, and that it would be a good idea to make it disappear.

It was to lessen the enormous disgrace that I felt for not

having succeeded, for still being alive, for having to suffer the shame of her having it her way again, that Bitch, and now she would be so sure that I had staged this scene for her so that she would come back to me. That would be a real curse, for sure.

I know that — had I succeeded — her victory would have been even greater ... but once I was dead, it wouldn't have bothered me at all.

Instead, here I am, unable to move for who knows how many more days, given that the bullet did not hit my heart but instead grazed my spinal column — without injuring my spinal nerve but leaving me in real danger of total paralysis to the upper limbs.

That's all I need, since I am bound to live.

And now the questions will start: "Why did you do it?", "Why did you continue to keep guns in the house?" and so forth and so on.

It's simple: I did it because I didn't want to live anymore and I kept — actually I keep — guns in the house because I collect guns.

I have always been a gun collector, ever since I was a first-year at university and I went around armed even to birthday parties. Just to show off, of course; especially to girls. Like that time with Francesca's cousin, who couldn't believe that I had a bullet loaded in the chamber.

She was a fifteen-year-old kid; I was nearly ten years older and didn't yet know that we would have a romance in a few years' time.

But who the hell cares about these memories ... even though, after all, they might even be pleasant ones, since they pertain to the life I had before meeting Francesca ... and ruination.

I've always wanted the best of everything, especially beautiful things, and it has been beautiful women that have brought me literally to ruin.

I've had pass through my hands a number of good matches (better and better), and they were all attractive young women whose parents, especially their mothers, competed to catch me. I've always had to be very careful so as not to find myself officially engaged without my knowledge, or nearly so. I recall that the only girl who didn't drag me home to meet her family (this is how it always starts) was exactly Elena, Francesca's cousin. But that was a few years later, with respect to that party where there was a shooting.

If only I had stayed by Elena's side instead of treating her so badly — dropping her for that other girl who was not as good looking, but in such a hurry to tie me down that she was willing to give in to me. Those were the old days when girls had reputations as 'good girls' or 'fast girls'.

If I think about how many interests I had in common with Elena, I must have been an idiot to let her go. I could say the same about myself later, during the whole time I watched Francesca slowly pulling away from me at the same rate as my ability to fulfil her every desire diminished.

With Elena I could talk about books as well — something of which my mother's house was always full and which my mother was always spurring us (my brothers and me) on to read. They were mostly international literature and, even though it is true that I was a huge failure at university, it is also a fact that reading has been an integral part of my life. And I owe all this to my mother. And, given the circumstances, it now occurs to me that it could easily have been her and not Ann Bronte who pronounced the notorious phrase — "The human heart is like india-rubber; a little swells it, but a great deal will not burst it. If 'little more than nothing' will disturb it, 'little less than all things will suffice' to break it." — a statement which like no other is an apt summary of my wickedly intense life, even though I wanted to blast my heart with a bullet — but that was only because it had already been broken by the heartache Francesca gave it.

Getting back to literature, even this shared interest could have drawn me to Elena; indeed it did keep us quite close for a long time when she, with her proverbial reasonableness, stayed friends with both Francesca and me, despite my previous behavior towards her.

Elena does not judge a book by its glossy and severely black cover, like those on the art magazines which Francesca has always strewn about the house.

"They appease my aesthetic senses, as objects of art," she used to say, and she even said it again during that last horrible argument we had in front of our friend 'the Shrink' and his girlfriend.

As for literature, well, whether it be the Bronte sisters or Baudelaire or a living Italian novelist — according to her, whether in prose or in verse, they were all writers of silly little stories for dreamy teenagers.

"How can anyone be interested in exploring feelings and all that sentimental stuff? I'm not interested in what goes on in anyone else's mind and I don't give a damn about what other people are feeling," she used to say all the time, and almost each and every time she saw me with a novel or a book of poetry in my hand. And it was quite often that she used to see me like that.

Why all of this is coming back to me, I don't know. I was thinking about Laura, the one that used sex to keep me by her side .... Well, she didn't manage to get me to the altar either because a few months later, I was invited to the eighteenth birthday party of a friend of my little sister and I didn't take her along with me to that.

I thought that I did not know the Birthday Girl and I didn't even want to go to the party (and if only I had never gone!) because I imagined that I would be a lonely Methuselah amongst teenagers and the under-twenty-ones.

Instead — worse luck for me — it was an exceptional evening and not only from the point of view of having fun. Some friends of Francesca's brother (the one who studied in Switzerland and was more or less my own age) had also been invited, but I didn't know that either before going to the party.

Elena was there, too, and that was when I discovered that

Francesca was her stunning little cousin, a few years younger than herself — the one she had told me about when we were still going out together, the one who she swore she would never introduce me to because I would surely have been the ruin of her. I remember that this had started a delicious skirmish between us, because Elena has a great sense of humor and I always liked her for this as well. I had shot back that I had never had any interest in minors because I didn't go looking for problems and that she could go ahead and keep her little jewel well hidden from me so that it wouldn't get ruined. And instead it was Francesca who ruined me.

That evening I witnessed the first of her breathtaking grand entrances. It was in a large room where for a few seconds everyone fell silent — literally without breathing — before breaking into deafening applause for the celebrant.

I was stunned for a couple of seconds, trying to remember whether that young blond goddess had already appeared to me in dreams or whether I had already encountered her in this world.

In her long periwinkle-blue sleeveless evening gown that bared her shoulders but allowed one to intuit a cleavage worthy of the expensive but refined diamond necklace which her parents had given her for the occasion, I could not immediately identify her with the elegant horsewoman who had appeared at the riding stables in that cloud of golden dust which her hair made against the sun. I'm sure that all those present belonging to the male sex were bewitched by that apparition, which was neither contrived nor excessive; the gown was of a simplicity and elegance appropriate for the young age of the person wearing it and for the circumstances.

It was beauty in its purest state. And tasteful.

For my own self, those two things have always carried the same weight because I think that they are completely integrated. I am an aesthete, for whom everything, even sex, must have those two qualities. I don't understand men who will grab anything; men who see themselves as hunters and therefore, just like the proverbial hunter, they feel that they mustn't be squeamish, but have to bag any prey before it has a chance to get away. On the contrary, can you really compare the pleasure of trapping a beautiful fox with just clutching a silly farmyard hen?

That evening was when my life began to go to the dogs, at Francesca's eighteenth birthday party, when I began at once to court her, notwithstanding her initial reluctance stemming from her being painfully shy. Yet it was her very bashfulness that betrayed her interest in me, a much older guy, experienced and rich. Each time our gazes crossed, her diaphanous skin could not hide the blush of pleasure which rose from her throat to her cheeks, and she would immediately look away without smiling.

I knew through my sister that there was a blonde girl in her class who was really cute but very unsociable. She said that the girl seemed to look down on most of the others, so she labeled her as an unlikeable asshole — it was Francesca she was talking about.

At once it was clear to me that I was dealing with a flower that had never been plucked and I found fascinating her slightly ungainly walk, and the way that she hunched her shoulders to hide her ample bosom. I know now that, had I left her wallowing in her own insecurities instead of stroking her ego like Pygmalion, I could have kept her all to myself to enjoy in our own private world.

Instead, soon I started to commit a series of errors (actually, always the same error stemming from my first erroneous evaluation) which allowed Francesca to grow her first pair of wings, before trying a trial flight close to home around the pair of us, before taking off for good in the distant future.

I quickly grasped that she came from a very privileged sector of society, not only economically advantaged, but also from an environment able to isolate itself from the common folk — from the norm, from people whom they considered to be ordinary.

But I also quickly realized that my reputation had, as usual, preceded me, and so there would be no need to show off my antique car parked in the villa's large courtyard from which I had regally descended, followed by my teetering younger sister who was unaccustomed to high heels.

The day after the party, at the end of classes, I was outside my sister's school, ready to give Francesca a ride home, too, should the occasion arise.

She accepted with her usual blush, and with that certain glint of interest in her grey eyes, eyes which immediately darted away from mine.

I was in the jeep from the stables, but it had been washed and waxed for the occasion. Naturally, I had taken some care with the interior: the dashboard gleamed, and the leather seats gave off that refined smell of the countryside and of beeswax, which I had instructed that day's stable boy to spray.

During the entire trip, which I managed to make last a whole forty minutes, Francesca said not a word except: "Another car … as nice as the one from yesterday".

We dropped her off in front of the gate to the villa, after the two girls had made arrangements to meet up at the cinema in the afternoon.

I immediately set my mind in motion and decided to offer to save my mother the trouble of yet again having to drive down to the city in order to take my sister there.

And to show off my luxury motorcycle.

Francesca was much more loquacious this time and, after I had turned off the motor, she immediately exclaimed "When will you take me for a spin on it?"

"Whenever you like," was my reply, said with studied non-chalance, the cause and effect of knowing that I had dealt her a masterstroke and impressed her no end.

Then it rained for three days straight, so there was no taking the motorcycle out for a ride. I nearly did a rain dance to placate the gods.

But there was no need, because on the fourth day I managed

to take the motorcycle out to pick my sister up from school. The sun was shining surreally in a sky as clear as never before — or was it just me that saw it that way because I had wanted it so much?

While I was waiting at the bottom of the staircase, I left the motor running, and even revved it slightly so that it would rumble a bit. And there they were, both of them, dashing headlong down the steps and smiling at me: my sister ready to jump on the rear seat and Francesca, not blushing at all, saying, "It's sunny today. At three o'clock in front of the gates to my house."

Not even a hint of "Would you like?", "Are you free?", or "If you could". Actually, now that I think about it through an association of ideas, one of my friends, who was mixed up for a while in a disastrous affair with Francesca's sister, said to me — about twenty years afterwards (just after our marriage had broken up, so that's a couple of years ago) — "Didn't you know that the Busi sisters never ask but always take?" And I was sure then and am still sure that he used the surname to emphasize the family's excessive sense of superiority. I here now state that I have never felt inferior to them because I have never been so, therefore despite his misery and rage, my friend's bitter quip didn't really register with me.

Anyway, getting back to the story about the three of us outside the school, I didn't make a case out of it, stupidly filled with pride and happy to have been saved the effort of having to invite her to go for this great ride we'd been talking about for so long.

I didn't know where her decisive tone came from — though I do now — and I put it down then to an adolescent need to appear grown up, and a need to hide her own sense of insecurity.

Moreover, I noticed that every day my sister was constantly reproached by my mother for never saying "please" before a request or "thank you" afterwards.

The ride itself was nothing special. Francesca couldn't stay out more than an hour because, she said, her sister was covering for her with the maid.

We went for a ride around the lake, and I brought her back safe and sound after exactly fifty-five minutes, bidding her farewell with a brotherly peck on the cheek.

When I promised her that I would pick her up from school the next day, she astonished me with the question "Which car will you drive?" To which I laughingly answered by saying that I would present myself on horseback. She did not laugh at my crack and I felt pretty awkward for having said it.

Amongst Francesca's negative qualities, there has always been her total lack of a sense of humor, however, at that time, I never noticed any defects.

Now that I think of it, in more than twenty years, I have never seen her laugh at a joke nor have I ever heard her tell one.

"It's not my style," she would say in a conceited tone, as though the whole thing were a vulgar display ... but even her arrogance could fascinate me.

As for the horse outside the school, while I was reassuring her that it was all a joke, I remember catching myself wondering how different she was from her cousin, who could bounce the verbal ball back into my court forever.

That's how our love story began — that is, as a relationship between me, an experienced man, with a beautiful girl who was both shy and cheeky, and who would stay like that in all respects, sex included, and who would intrigue me to the point where I would marry her within just a few years.

The error of evaluation I made with her was to have wanted her with all my being as resolutely as I had wanted all the other lovely girls before her, considering myself lucky to have found a jewel of even greater value, but to have never noticed the huge difference between the way that the others had loved me back and how she did.

As with all the previous girls, all more or less the same age as me except for Elena, Francesca was attracted to my being well-off, but because she was inexpert and insecure, unable to fairly compare, she too chose me on blind faith, so to say.

For her, to sit in my luxury cars, to be taken to the most

fashionable restaurants and discotheques, to note with what marvelous solicitude she was greeted and treated in the exclusive boutiques where I took her to pick out her presents — this was all part of the fairy-tale life of riches and luxury which so much affects most people. And from the very beginning, she wanted to be part of that picture, which did not surprise me at all.

The thing which would take me some good time to discover was her congenital avidity.

In the beginning, I mistook for innocence the fact that she did not seem to notice that it was she herself, with her beauty and her being so much younger than me, that made people marvel, and that fascinated shop assistants and head waiters alike. They had always been very polite to me, but never as deferential nor as nearly servile.

And as a consequence of my initial error, I made an even more serious one in the following years. While I was busy spoiling her, I did not take into consideration the danger I was courting by always telling her how beautiful she was, and by letting her know how well she satisfied my inner erotic world which depended so much on the beautiful.

I think that, though she came from a very wealthy background, when she found herself surrounded, or rather submerged, by my presents and by the attention which were offered (always as the homage due to the woman of my dreams), it kept her from being able to evaluate how much, or even if, she would have liked me had I been without all my economic means.

Economic means which lasted for some fifteen years, after which came a less florid period, which then debouched into hard times. At that point, she had already begun to fly about here and there "in search of innocent fulfillment" as she used to reassure me when I asked her where she had disappeared to for ever-longer lapses in time. Suddenly she informed me that all of these difficulties that we were going through were causing her immense stress and that she had found a modestly-priced psychoanalyst, whose sessions were making her feel better.

When, shortly afterwards, she left me, she found a thousand different and contradictory reasons why our marriage had ended.

The only real reason was that she had ended up in his claws, notwithstanding he had shamelessly boasted about our couples being friends.

As a matter of fact, although we did hang out together for a while, always the four of us, I hadn't understood that those friendly conversations in restaurants or in each other's houses were what he needed in order to let Francesca know the details about his life which would otherwise be difficult for him to bring up during their therapy sessions in his study.

When I recall that we even talked about literature — the two of them and myself, of course — my blood boils with the thought of what a great deceiver he was: he had perfectly understood what was the only point in which I did not feel fulfilled by Francesca and he offered "as a friend" to fill that void.

Evidently he had also identified all of Francesca's weak points and he knew how to use them to his advantage, because when he was with me he lavished praise on her intelligence and on her "receptiveness to more rational and scientific matters", and he made sure to always do this within earshot of Francesca. He constantly pointed out how lucky I was to have a wife with such a complete personality, even though I was still mainly as impressed by her exterior appearance as I had been the first day I had set eyes on her.

Evidently that was not the only weak point that he had identified in Francesca, because often, and with apparent modesty, he spoke of his properties and of the inheritance which he would come into only after a few years.

Or he would nonchalantly ask his then companion how many square meters the lounge was in the villa by the sea.

This woman, who was also a friend of ours, seemed to be perennially bewitched by him, enchanted by the voice that came out of that shaved dome. It must have been a case of subjugation, I found myself thinking each time. And perhaps that is why I never realized that the snake charmer had turned his gaze elsewhere.

The evening that they turned up in the latest model of Maserati, I saw Francesca run towards it, rather than towards our guests who were climbing out of it.

I realized that it was all over between us ... given that my numerous cars had been cut down to just one large Volvo, in which Francesca could still cut a grand figure.

It was that evening that Francesca and I had a ferocious altercation about her artistic feelings being fulfilled by glossy magazines, and about how bored she was to see me absorbed in reading my mother's old books.

Her analyst said that we were both right ... but I didn't like that intimate gesture with which he dried a tear from her eye.

Chapter Three
Elena's Error of Evaluation

I don't think that I have ever had an experience even remotely similar to that in which I found myself after getting together again with my cousin Francesca.

I used the expression "get together with" rather than "get close to", because our language can be subtle indeed, and this difference might never be noticed by even the most expert of foreign linguists.

It's true that we usually say "get together with" when we want to express the idea that two poles have moved closer to each other, whereas when we mean a reciprocal interest and the will to maintain contact, we would use "get close to".

It wasn't like that, my cousin and I finding each other again. At the time, I underestimated her initial coolness when she answered the phone, mistaking it for astonishment. It was me who had wanted this — wanted her to hear my voice for the first time in ten years and on her new number as well, since she had never given me that phone number — yet she needed no persuading and demonstrated nothing more than genuine surprise.

Not that she had ever tried to make herself unreachable. It was simply that she had erased me — "suppressed" me as she would explain later, using language more appropriate to her changed status.

Her life, in fact, had changed completely during that long stretch of time, even though it is true that the turning point in her life — cohabiting with a new partner — had been fairly recent. Francesca and Massimo had separated. She had suddenly abandoned the marital roof two years ago.

My initial mistake consisted exactly in thinking that her choice was her redeeming (and I didn't care how late) twenty years of living like a featherbrain, at the mercy of a man who had nullified her ability to think for herself, by slowly instilling in her the certainty that her looks alone made the world turn round. He had convinced her that, because of that great gift of God, people would rush to grant her every desire and that she need only knock for every door to be opened for her. Neither would she ever need to try any other doors, because he could bestow success on her on any day and at any hour. No other proof was needed, because his very own sense of Good Taste was the hardest test she would ever have to face, and in that arena she had already scored top marks. By following his advice, she passed the grade every day.

But I would soon discover that Francesca did still have a few other mental faculties left which could be annihilated, and that her new partner had done so with a completely different technique.

Anyway, getting back to Massimo, he added as proof of the validity of his argument the fact that he had always been able to pull the prettiest and most desirable girls in his social circle, and that the only reason she hadn't known this fact was because she had been too young at the time. But hadn't she herself quickly noted with what perfect ease he moved in Society and how many possibilities were open to him in life because of this?

With this kind of brainwashing going on, and by making her every wish come true (while the money lasted), he had not only spoiled Francesca, he had also made the idea take root in her that good looks alone were enough to be a success in life.

Notwithstanding the few instances which belied this during the time when we first used to go around together — that is, our whole lives before we fell out— when I wanted to get back in touch with Francesca, I realized that she was still paddling about in the murky depths of complacency. Waters which had become even more perilous since her new man, who was even more sly than her husband had been, had got her to believe also that it was her powers of intellect as well as her stunning beauty which would make her life easy. Something which might even be absolutely true, though never in the the labour market, where a formal degree is also required.

In short, he had reinforced an idea that had snaked all through her marriage — that a formal degree of any kind was not necessary.

Thinking back on it now, this enormous lie was nothing more than a rare instance of his regurgitation of something consistent with his own successful choices in life, which had lead him to become a professional "spellbinder" whose magic was no more than a smokescreen of words. But, back then, not even Francesca could have known that.

When I found her again, Francesca, who was only a little younger than me, was about to turn fifty and the idea of working did not even occur to her.

It would take at least another two years of chatting with me before she felt even a twinge of desire for independence — and also because she had found herself in straitened circumstances.

Anyway it would only ever be no more than a twinge.

I had to accept the twofold idea that Francesca's inner self had by now been completely shaped by the two craftsmen of her destiny, who had operated on the two levels of her mind — so similar to each other but different. Even though the men seemed to be in conflict with each other, evidently they both had found themselves working on the same easily plowed terrain, completely lacking in that vital seed, which is a respect for others and for oneself, and lacking in the capacity to see beyond physical features.

Francesca has no conscience, and like all other persons similar to her, she does not care about others nor have any morals;

I had never even come close to this thought in the many years (literally a lifetime) that we had known each other.

That was the thing that I had got so colossally wrong when I wanted us to be reconciled. I had completely absolved her for the hurt she had caused me ten years ago, blaming her 'only' for the wrong of letting herself be dragged by her husband into the vortex of spite that he had heaped on me during those last two days of August which we had spent on my then partner's sailing boat.

I remember that we had prepared that trip to Sardinia down to the smallest detail a few days after introducing him to them, and that what happened in the forty-eight hours after their arrival on board was something incredible. Even now, it still seems incredible to me, though by now I do know how profound were the underlying reasons.

Francesca and I had got straight to work storing the provisions and we were chatting in a light-hearted way about the sudden change of behavior in Massimo, who, with each minute that passed, seemed to be taking on more and more the likeness of my partner Carlo. The thing made us smile and it was in fact Francesca who said, "This morning he asked me to get out those Lacoste polo shirts that I had bought him years ago and that he never wore because he only wears his tailor-made shirts". I was amazed by her ironic, nearly sneering, tone because I had always thought that they were on the same wavelength when it came to clothes.

"They look like old friends," I said and added, "Just as well, because it means that the crew is tight. That is so important on a ship. You'll notice that" (though she would never have had the time to, given the events that unfolded in the few hours around midday). And I wouldn't know how to reconstruct the events exactly because everything seemed to tumble surreally as in a fantasy after my accident.

I had turned towards the dinette, intending to clean the table before laying out a light meal to eat before casting off, when I tripped over a case of bottled mineral water which shouldn't have been there. I fell forwards and in grabbing for the edge of the table, I dragged off the breadknife that I had only just placed there and I ended up with it stabbed into my wrist.

At that point, everything seemed to fast forward: the bleeding wouldn't stop, so Carlo wrapped something around my arm and loaded me into the car to dash off, horn blaring, to a hospital in the nearest city.

He was very sweet to me and I don't know how many times he repeated that he wouldn't leave without me, but that he was sure that once I had been treated, I would still be able to enjoy the cruise, and he added:

"Thank goodness that we invited them. This way, if need be, Francesca can spare you some of the work in the kitchen. They seem to have understood that All Hands set to on a ship, especially if there is someone on board who doesn't feel well. Massimo can't wait to get his hands on the ropes and sails — or at least, that's what it looks like to me. And Francesca was a big help with you after changing out of that ridiculous outfit she arrived in. I won't pretend that I wasn't somewhat perplexed ... she made me think of Princess Di, although the shipping magnate in question wasn't called Dodi, was he, my Love?"

Carlo tried every which way to play down the worrisome situation.

Fortunately, the tendon was not damaged, but given that the wound was deep and had taken three stitches, the doctor ordered me not to set sail before the case had been reviewed. We were supposed to report back to the hospital the next morning. So we went back to the boat and Carlo said that we would have to spend the night there, unless they wanted to stay more comfortably at home and come back on board the next morning at the same time.

"No problem," said Massimo immediately, with the air of someone who is accustomed to commanding a crew. "The patient can lay in the shade of the awning I put up when you were away, here on the mats and cushions that Francesca has arranged in the cockpit. We've even made something to eat. We'll moor here tonight."

Carlo and I surreptitiously looked at each other and I think that the same thought crossed both our minds. What had happened in the two-and-a-half hours that we had been away?

Massimo seemed to be completely at ease in his role of second-in-command and more resolute in his actions, yet in the days leading up to our cruise and even up until just before I had my accident, he had always seemed to look for Carlo's approval, even if the question wasn't explicit. "So much the better," I said to myself, concerned that I might be a burden in my present condition.

Not now though. Having screened that film clip in my head over and over for years, I am neither perplexed nor do I believe that I should have felt relieved when we were living that moment.

The process of identification with Carlo was completing itself in Massimo's mind, and that did not bode at all well.

In fact, if the workings of his mind had limited itself to a kind of light transfer, things would not have happened as they indeed did.

Instead, after that small silly episode about polo shirts, which had made us women share a smile, Massimo had more and more identified himself with Carlo, to the point that he wanted Carlo all to himself as a friend and had even tried to push me away from what he wanted to become his own exclusive circle of favorites.

In fact, as I was falling asleep, stunned by tranquilizers, I just managed to mentally note something he said to Carlo.

"You are so lucky: you have a beautiful boat, a satisfying career and an adorable kid to have fun with at sea". He was alluding to Carlo's son, Antonio. Of me, not a mention.

It was that sentence which, during the ten years of the break in our relationship, I had considered as proof that Francesca was innocent of foul play towards me.

In fact, that was not the end of it.

The next morning, Carlo set the table for breakfast in the dinette, so that we could all share a meal before taking me back to the hospital. And that is when Massimo manifested in full his process of identification with Carlo, which evidently in his mind had already arrived at the phase of project planning. "If I were you, I wouldn't strive for anything more in life. I'd sail off on the waves with my son and just the air and the sun would be enough for me," Massimo said, looking straight at me.

Why had he not included me in this idyllic portrait of Carlo's life?

Carlo did not seem to notice the verbal vacuum, but I, with Massimo's eyes staring into mine, understood that it was not just thoughtlessness, and I felt offended.

After a moment, Carlo simply said: "And with Elena, of course. Isn't that true, Antonio? We're not leaving her ashore, are we?"

The boy agreed with a smile and Carlo put his arm around my shoulders and said that it was time to go.

In the car, Carlo asked me if I didn't also think that Massimo was acting a bit strange, but he was only alluding to his behavior as the perfect organizer the afternoon and evening before. So, Carlo had noticed, too. And the fact that he had answered back after the insult to me meant that I did not have to dwell on the theme of what a pleasant life he could enjoy by going off to sea.

We arrived at the hospital still joking about Massimo but we departed saddened because I was still forbidden to sail, since the surgeon had held that the wound needed to be dressed by medical experts and also that life aboard a ship would not be hygienic enough.

We could see that all our plans had been ruined, and Carlo asked himself how Antonio would take it, since he'd been talking happily about sighting the coast at dawn, and maybe even sighting a pirate ship.

Without hesitating, I told Carlo that he should not deprive the boy of this holiday he had so been looking forward to, and I told him how Antonio had told me that he was going to spend hours at the helm with his father. I would stay ashore and they should cast off with Francesca and Massimo.

But Carlo was just as swift to swear that while he would do everything he could so as not to disappoint Antonio, he would convince him that it was necessary to put off the sail. He would take Antonio for a walk along the pier as soon as we arrived so as to be alone with him.

That's what he did, and they were just coming back on board, relaxed and ready to tell us something, but before they could, Massimo went up to them and said: "But why should he suffer just because Elena has hurt herself and can't leave with you (he didn't say "us")? Francesca can take her home while we re-organize the departure."

Carlo looked at him aghast, then looked at me and said curtly "Antonio and I have decided that even though we are very sorry for our guests, that we will put off this cruise for two weeks. That way Elena can join us. You and Francesca are invited again, naturally," and then softening his voice, he said "Right, Antonio?"

The boy looked at me affectionately and ran over to hug me.

I was proud of them and even more perplexed by Massimo's behavior, incomprehensible to me, especially since he knew how much I was in love with Carlo.

And Francesca knew that very well, too. But the worst was yet to come.

We sat down to talk about our newly changed plans while Francesca served us a snack. Very soon after that our friendship would come to an end. I can now add that the relationship with my cousin would be interrupted for the next ten years.

In fact, after not having said more than perhaps a dozen words since she had arrived on board the day before, Francesca was now particularly loquacious and she surprised me by how she wanted to give her opinion about my relationship with

Carlo — a subject that had nothing at all to do with the interest at hand. Evidently the two of them had conferred, Massimo and Francesca, and she had fervently adopted her husband's opinion. At least that was my conclusion at the time, even if I did not forgive her for it.

Since her intervention had not a thing to do with the general discussion, I remember that Carlo looked at her somewhat perplexed while she spoke. On a par with her husband, she was unusually full of initiative, serving drinks and describing her sandwich fillings. Suddenly and very nonchalantly, she said "Carlo, I only knew you from what Elena had told us about you, but in these few hours that we've been together I can see that you two are quite different from each other. I find that you are quite anomalous as a couple. I was thinking about it this morning while you two were at the hospital. I may be wrong, but I don't think it's going to last between the two of you."

And then she shut up, convinced, and as definite as a death sentence on my love with Carlo. Obviously she had no power over us, but I simply could not accept such behavior from her, unless it could be explained by the fact that by then her subjugation to Massimo was total. And even if it had been no more than her aping him, she had carried it off perfectly, using the same peremptory assertive tone of voice as her husband, something which had already amazed Carlo and I.

Francesca's treacherous words hit me like a violent stab in the back, and I decided at that very moment to never see her again.

Whether it had been undue influence or stupid imitation, the two of them had gone beyond the pale with me, even though I stayed convinced for the next ten years that the *deus ex machina* had been Massimo.

So it was with this in mind, and with Carlo in agreement, that we went back home from Portofino. Even Antonio had been struck by their words, because suddenly, as often happens with children who seem to not be paying attention to the adult conversation around them, he asked me "Elena, didn't you say that you wanted them to come with us to Sardinia because they were your friends — I mean, relatives?"

Carlo and I looked at each other without knowing quite how to answer, and then he came to my rescue by telling him that sometimes you don't really know people and that they can give you a nasty surprise, but that this would never happen to the three of us. That seemed to satisfy him.

And, in fact, we went back to Portofino two weeks later, but only the three of us.

Well, notwithstanding all the ugliness we had gone through then, once Francesca was separated from Massimo, I forgave her everything and looked her up again, but I would pay a dear price for my error of evaluation within two years of our new start, when I would help her escape from the second tyrant of her mind, the Charmer she had introduced me to.

I believed again that I had to free her from that other dependency. Instead, I had to accept the idea that in both cases, the two men were no more than litmus papers dipped into Francesca's soul where there was no morality at all.

I had repeated the same error of evaluation because for all my life up till that moment, I had not wanted to acknowledge the meanness of a person who was so dear to me. I should never have looked her up again.

Chapter Four
The Story

"How lovely to be home again. I won't deny it: I loved to travel, I love my job, but this time I was really fed up with being away from home. I would have come back six months ago, but it wasn't up to me."

"How long were you away this time? Two years? Three?" her brother asked her. "I missed you."

"I missed you, too, you know. Time flies, Handsome. It was four years — a pretty long 'away match', as my boss would say. And to think that at the beginning he said that I wouldn't need to be there more than six months or so — eight at the most. Believe me, I couldn't stand it anymore. All I ever dreamed about was to come back and see you again, to see everybody, to just get my old life back again. But, hey, tell me the latest. I feel like I did when I went away to college and I was missing out on everything."

"Oh, sure! All you ever did was extol your life out of the clutches of Mummy and Daddy. I could have died of envy over the freedom you had. Now I swear that this is the first time that I have ever heard you say that you missed home and running around with us."

"Well, that was a good while ago, wasn't it? Maybe I see it differently now and maybe I remember it wrong. Anyway, shoot! Tell me all."

"Elena, not much ever happens here, you know that. The same old stuff: work and commuting. My job is pretty sedentary and between the office and the courtroom, it's not like I have a lot of fun or meet a lot of people. Plus, I have a family, right? We can't really take many trips, so, except for taking the usual vacations, the only time I ever travel is when it is for work. And I sure don't go as far away as you do. How is it going with the Agency? After you stayed there such an awfully long time getting that holiday village (wasn't it?) up and running, are they going to give you that job you wanted?"

"I think so because everyone is really happy with the job I did, especially the Boss. But I asked you to bring me up to date with what's happening here. How come you changed the subject?"

"Because I already told you that nothing ever happens here. And anyway, you and I have always been like that, haven't we? Do you remember in high school? We'd come home for lunch and Mamma would ask us 'How was school today?' and I would always answer, 'Okay' and then you would start spouting tons of stuff that you knew that Mamma would be interested in and it was always stuff that I had no idea that was going on around me."

"Clearly it was the usual guy–gal difference. Now, think! Four years is a long time. Can it be that there were no marriages or divorces amongst our friends and acquaintances — no grandchildren born? I've really been out of touch, even if I did have the internet."

"Hmmn, let me think... Oh, yeah. But surely you heard about it. It was a bombshell two or three years ago: Francesca and Massimo split up. It was totally out of the blue. I mean, you can imagine ... after twenty years of marriage."

"No, I certainly did not know! Well, I mean, who bothered to tell me? You certainly didn't let me know and we were always in touch."

"You're right, but I suppose that I didn't think it was all that important. We always had plenty of other things to pass along the telephone line between Italy and Kenya. And anyway, you know what? I really never gave a damn about those two. If she weren't our cousin, I would have lost sight of her years ago when we were in high school. That's what I say."

"Wait … let me guess: she found him in bed with someone else, right? 'The leopard cannot change his spots' the old saying goes, and after all, we are talking about the years of marriage being twenty."

"No, actually, it was the opposite. She dumped him and she took up with one of their friends. Massimo was absolutely desperate about it."

"What? No way! They were so in love, and she used to hang on his every word."

"Yes, exactly. And you know what I've always thought about how she managed to hang on his every word. That little slut of our cousin latched onto a meal ticket on her eighteenth birthday and never let it go."

"What do you mean? Aren't you exaggerating a bit? It's not like all rich couples marry for money, you know. After all, even our aunt and uncle are well-to-do, aren't they?"

"True. Nobody knows how true love is born and how this is different from just having a crush and so on."

"Listen, you well know that I haven't seen her in ten years. But it seemed to me that she was always totally addicted to Massimo — you remember what happened that time on the sailboat, right? Say what you like, but something really bad must have happened between them, and it couldn't just be down to some romantic encounter that Francesca had."

"What happened was that the 'Eternal Fountain of Love' dried up."

"What does that mean?"

"Oh, really … are you being stupid or just playing dumb? It's all very well that you've been away for four years, but even ten years ago when there was that ruined sailing trip, you must have known that business wasn't going too well for Massimo. It was you who told me about it, wasn't it?"

"Oh, yeah; that's true. Now I remember … he couldn't afford to buy a sailing boat. But what's that got to do with it?

I don't see how you can be so sure about that being the reason for their break-up."

"Well then, let's see if it all adds up. From that time onwards, according to what I heard at the time, the bread got more and more scarce. And as the bottomless pit of cash got more and more shallow, higher and higher were the number of fights and the number of flights when Francesca would take off and disappear. As I remember, he even came looking for her at our place a couple of times."

"And then what happened?"

"Nothing. Overnight she was gone. She took off with a guy from one of the couples that they were friends with. And Massimo shot himself."

"Oh my God! And you say that like it was nothing more than him going out and getting drunk. Did he die?"

"Oh no, no, no. But you should see him — he's a mere shadow of the Massimo we used to know ... that guy that used to ride around on a horse ... the one who used to court you."

"That sure is a lot of water under the bridge. I am so sorry to hear all this. He always was a lady-killer, I mean, up until he met Francesca. But to think of him as being dead .... And how is he?"

"How do you suppose he is? Without a wife and without a dime. When you think about the life he used to live and the way he kept our cousin... I thank God that I never met a woman like her. When she was young, you could see that she would be a great beauty, but very greedy, too."

"At this point, I couldn't say if you are right or wrong. I think that he was the one who pulled her strings any way he wanted to, right from the start. Maybe that was the image that we all had — Massimo the Big Shot — which helped a good deal with her ... and his money, too. But I think that she really was totally in his thrall ... to the point that she even spoke like him. When I think back to those forty-eight hours on the sailboat, it makes me sick. That helpless anger I felt then still washes over me — when I wanted to shout in her face that she had become as arrogant and rude as he was. But then, on second thought, his manners always were very aristocratic, weren't they? I didn't shout because of the longstanding friendship the three of us had. It was that more than the fact that we were related. You know that I chose to stop seeing them rather than to have to spell out for them just how insulting they had been towards me. Actually, it was Carlo who they should have thanked, really, because I was too offended and furious. Anyway I'm still of the same opinion that it was all his doing. Even this latest mess that you are telling me about, too. You know that I stayed friends with Massimo (and then of course with the both of them) in spite of the way he treated me when I was twenty. I was so upset when he just stated loud and clear to me that Laura was ready to give in to him and that he was more than willing to amuse himself with her. He was cold and cynical, as though he were simply announcing his intention to change jobs to something more productive."

"You certainly picked a good comparison — a job — for someone who has never worked in his life. I would have said that it was more like what he would have done with one of his cars, don't you think?"

"You're right. And to think that I put it all down to the ignorance of youth, even though he was a little older than me."

"So when you ran into him with Francesca a few years later, is that why you pretended that nothing had happened? I always wondered how you could just forget all the times you cried because of him, even in front of me."

"You know that I never tie a string around my finger to remember something. Not like you! What's the point of going over and over the past, when you know that life goes on. Thank God that we grow up and mature. Even now, for example, I think that I just might get in touch with Francesca. After all, she's not only my cousin, but she used to be one of my best friends."

"Well, aren't you a clever girl! 'To err is human, but to forgive is divine', I always say. Anyway, do what you want — you're a consenting adult. And do forgive all these clichés, but I think that you are blundering about like Shakespeare's Fool."

"I see that literary references do not pass you by, Sir. Admit it now: you can see that time has proved me right and that Massimo has failed with her as well."

"Okay, but what does Massimo have to do with it? Surely he's the same as he always was: a spoiled brat. But why do you want to go looking for that idiot who insulted you ten years ago?"

"You are right, you have every reason to say so. But, knowing him, I am convinced that besides being a spoiled brat (like you said), that he really knew how to control her. And even if he lost all his influence when his money gave out (and that is something which does no credit to Francesca), you still have to admit that she was very vulnerable."

"'Stupid' is what I think that you meant to say. You know that my opinion is the exact opposite of yours. Maybe it's because I'm a man. But for me, like I said before, it's all down to his having no worldly goods. But let's not get into it again. You do what you like and good luck to you. I certainly never missed her and she's been a pain in the neck ever since she was a kid, her head full of silly notions and always gossiping about the hicks she had to go to school with and one classmate or another who had no dress sense. Luckily, since she's been living with that other guy, it seems that she's been a real recluse and hasn't kept in touch with anyone. But I will add that, beautiful or not, I wouldn't touch her with a barge pole for all the tea in China. And look what's happened: in the five minutes that we've been talking about her, I've managed to utter every possible hackneyed phrase. Doesn't that say something about it all? As far as I am concerned, it's the oldest story in the book: when the wolf comes in through the door, love goes out of the window. Get it? Anyway, about giving you her number, I really should ask her first, don't you think? What with all that fuss between you ten years ago…"

"Well then, do it right away but don't tell her that I'm back here. You haven't changed at all. That's another reason why I wanted to come home. When I was down in Nairobi, our quick chats over the phone just weren't enough."

Elena and her brother were very close, and ever since high school, they had always run around with the same crowd because they were in the same age group.

After Elena's four-year absence working abroad, and despite emails and phone calls and texting, they still wanted to see each other in person and talk face-to-face while they waited for Renato's wife, before going out to dinner to celebrate Elena's return. There was just enough time to write down Francesca's new telephone number before the EntryPhone buzzed, interrupting their rather lively (as was usual for them) conversation.

At the restaurant, the time simply flew between laughter and wine and Elena's recounting of her travels, being interrupted now and again with information on who and what was happening among friends and acquaintances.

The whole time though, Elena's mind was churning over the 'bombshell' (as Renato called it), and she became ever more convinced that she would make use of that telephone number the very next morning because, after all, she was fond of Francesca. She had always been fond of her.

So, the next day — since, anyway, she had to go to the area where her cousin now lived — she took out of her handbag the post-it note on which Renato had written down the number, and she dialed it.

"Ciao," said Francesca after hesitating for a few seconds. "A pleasure. No, you're not interrupting anything. I was just surprised … it's been such a long time…"

"I'm just back from abroad and I heard about the big change in your life. I thought I might get back in touch, so I asked Renato for your new number."

"Yes. Yes, I know. He called me to ask if it was okay."

"And obviously you told him it was. Thanks. You know, I always thought that whatever happened back then was all because of the negative influence that Massimo had on you.

Look, to put it in a nutshell: if you would like to see me, I'm available, since I know that you two have separated and you're living with someone else now."

"Oh, yes. Things are fine now. I'm happy and my life is settled. You did the right thing to call me. I'd love to introduce you to him, so when would you like to come over?"

"Listen — the sooner I see you, the happier I will be. How about tomorrow morning? I have a couple of hours free between two appointments and I'll be in the neighborhood where Renato says you live now. It would be great if I could stop by for coffee."

"Okay. What time would be good for you?"

"Eleven o'clock would be perfect for me. How about you — I mean, for the two of you?"

"Yes, great, I can introduce him to you then because he'll be free between one session and another. By the way, did you know that he was a psychiatrist?"

"No, Renato didn't say. He only told me that you are living with someone."

"How odd, because he's someone that you notice, you see."

"Well," said Elena, a little put off by her cousin's stupid remark, "maybe it's because I didn't ask him for any details since I expected that you would fill me in. Anyway, you know how men are. And speaking of men, as far as I am concerned, it was good enough for me to hear that you had got yourself free of Massimo, so that's why I didn't ask about anything else. Well, now you know."

"Alright, alright ... we'll talk about it some other time," was the curt reply with which Francesca cut short the reference to her ex-husband.

"Just tell me if you really are happy."

"I'm in Seventh Heaven. You'll see: he's a charmer."

"As long as you don't introduce me to someone with a turban on his head and a flute to charm snakes..."

They had both laughed. It had been a long time since Francesca had laughed that way, but Elena couldn't have known that then.

"We've found each other again," thought Elena as they exchanged a friendly "'Bye" after arranging for her to go to Francesca's house the next day at eleven o'clock. Francesca had not hesitated in giving her the new address and that measure of trust had warmed her heart and given her hope for the revival of their friendship.

Elena found the idea of the 'charmer' intriguing and she was sure that Francesca must by now have finally opened her eyes to the inanity with which Massimo was 'blessed', hidden beneath the dash with which he had always fascinated everyone, her included. It could only be like that.

It was a cold February morning and the trees along the lane by the gate were leafless and sad. A pale sun filtered through low clouds which, blown by a fitful breeze, seemed to want to disappear from one moment to the next.

But the house was warm and welcoming — even beautiful — decorated with antiques from the entrance throughout, with nice rugs and a few modern pieces placed knowledgeably here and there. The whole design was an exceptional example of good taste and eccentricity, and showcased Francesca's unique style. Elena recognized a few pieces of furniture, unmistakable for their rare beauty, which she must have brought with her.

Her cousin's voice had sounded cordial over the EntryPhone, and when Elena entered the driveway to park her car on the wide apron of grey stones, she saw the door open beyond the lawn and the familiar figure of Francesca appear: tall, slim and dressed just as she had always been in the warm tones of brown and leather. Even at that distance Elena noticed that she was wearing riding boots, and she wondered if Francesca was about to go out or if she had just come back. Then a thought from the distant past coursed through her mind: perhaps it was only her habit of creating an appearance, of making an impression, to always see herself through the eyes of other people.

With a little shared embarrassment, they kissed each other's cheeks, hugged each other warmly, then immediately entered the kitchen.

"Sit down. Let's right away have something hot, shall we? The weather today…" said Francesca.

"Yes, thanks. I'd love that. It's great to see you again."

"I'm happy to see you again, too. I'm so glad that you called me. Now tell me, would you prefer coffee or a proper Japanese tea. I promise that I'll spare you the whole Ceremony — I learned how to do it on a course I took at the Japanese Cultural Institute."

Nope, Francesca had not changed.

"No, no, our own Italian espresso would be fine. I'm more interested in sitting down with you so that we can talk. Let's catch up, shall we?"

"Of course. And also because I believe that you've discovered that my news is a real sea change, right?"

The kitchen was large and very comfortable, with a sofa in front of a fireplace. The table was in the corner between two enormous glass sliding doors that opened onto a large terrace where more doors gave onto other rooms. Notwithstanding the uncertain weather, there was a lovely ambient light which struck the eye of anyone coming from the rather gloomy entrance, presently illuminated by a Tiffany lamp on the console table.

Even the kitchen appliances were out of the ordinary — somewhat affected but tasteful in their rounded shapes that reflected the light, increasing the effect.

"I see that you've done a lot of decorating" Elena said.

"Yes, but not the kitchen. This is his kingdom, and it was all like this when I moved in. I was surprised, too, some time ago when he proudly told us that his partner had had nothing to do with this part of the house. And she was present when he said it."

"Wow. You would never think that a man had created it. It's practical but intimate and comfortable."

"And none of his partners had a part in it. There have been three other women before me."

Elena hadn't replied but had merely looked around her

before concentrating her gaze on the table. It didn't seem to be set for a simple morning coffee break.

"But I see that your talent for setting a beautiful and extravagant table hasn't changed. Indeed, I'd say that you've managed to embellish it all."

"Thank you. He's crazy about that and he's always saying that this was a kingdom without a queen until I arrived. Apparently the other women limited themselves to the usual tablecloths — pretty but soulless — lacking that creativity that this place deserves. When I think back to what a scene Massimo made ... do you remember? It was that Christmas when I had set "a table fit for a funeral wake in an American film" and just because there was nothing red or silver or gold. Really, to say it in just a few words, it was only because I hadn't decorated our table according to the White Christmas theme that was everywhere present in his mother's house."

"Okay, but you have to agree with me that you'd gone a little over the top with the dark tones. Even your own mother asked you very tactfully why you hadn't chosen candles in a contrasting color to the festoons you decorated the tablecloth with — they were black, as I remember."

"True. Anyway, that was the only time that Massimo ever criticized my interior decorating. He was crazy about my soft furnishings, too, and I have to say that he always treated me as though I were an Architect or a successful Stylist."

"Speaking of which, what have you got to say about him? Renato told me about his desperate act."

"Yes, and just thinking about it makes me indignant. He's been going around saying that it's all my fault that his life turned out the way it did. And at the same time he says that he didn't shoot himself over me but instead he would have had to shoot himself if I had gone back to him."

"It all seems so absurd," said Elena in a neutral tone.

"The fact is that after telling me for twenty years that he found it inebriating (his words exactly) my way of decorating and my interest in art and especially in architecture, it turns out in the end that he actually couldn't stand it anymore to see me spend any money … squander (to use his words exactly again). Well, let's talk about it some other time."

At that moment, Marco came in as though it were by chance and as if he hadn't realized that there was a guest present.

"Am I interrupting anything?" he asked.

And Francesca replied "Not at all. Instead, come and meet Elena. I mentioned her to you yesterday."

"Ah, yes. I had forgotten. Excuse me."

Without getting up, Elena had spontaneously put out her hand in a friendly way, saying simply "I'm very pleased to meet you, sir." And when Francesca immediately corrected her by saying that formal address was not called for, she had shaken his hand warmly, having already totally associated him in her unprejudiced mind with the affection she felt for her cousin, and she had looked into his eyes with her own sincere green ones.

"We were talking about Massimo," said Francesca (as if he, who had been listening in from the wings, had needed any information). "Naturally it would be inevitable for Elena and me after all this time. We were remembering — or rather it was me — how we didn't always share my flights of fantasy. My 'lightness of being' as you call it."

"I was just saying that her creative talent hasn't changed," said Elena enthusiastically. "Anyway, I do find you much changed, much more sure of yourself and not just a mirror image of someone else's reflection."

"You've ascertained the correct diagnosis, I have to say" declared Marco with the voice of an expert. "Francesca has finally found herself."

It was obvious that Francesca was filled with joy as she saw the encounter transform itself into a celebration of her good taste and intelligence. Those words, pronounced and shared by her man and by her newly rediscovered Elena, were another confirmation of her worth. She was not in the least discomfited by Elena's explicit allusions to the way she had behaved in their 'previous life'. Which Elena understood.

They drank their coffee and Marco left, mentioning an urgent work issue.

"Getting back to Massimo," Francesca took up again, "I got the feeling that I was only a pretty object that he owned. If I think about how for years I was so captivated by the power I had over him... The effect I have on Marco is different, totally, and much more complete. If it had been him in place of Massimo, I think that by now I would have got somewhere professionally — not that work is indispensable if there are other means of support. You know, one thing that I love about Marco is that being the expert that he is, he literally adores me for my intellectual abilities. Life with him is a constantly enriching education. Just think — he is so convinced and supportive that he lets me run our group of self-knowledge and confrontation. You know what I'm talking about, right?"

"Sure, I know what you mean. And at the moment I'm actually looking for something like that. Who knows, maybe I'll ask you for more details. But we have plenty of time to talk about it again, right? So, tell me more about what we were talking about before", said Elena.

"I was telling you that the group is 'ours', you see? And I am not just one of the participants — the patients, if you like — but we ourselves run it together — I run it with him as a co-leader. You can't imagine how I love to study and delve into it all... And primarily to exchange ideas with him and then us together with the group. They really listen to me and the fact that he holds me so much in esteem means that they can trust that I know what I am doing, even if I don't have a degree. You see how I was right — how we were right (I mean Massimo and I) — to think that a university degree is useless and that professors often know less than we do." After Francesca got all this out, she said with a questioning tone, "Do you get what I'm saying?"

Elena understood perfectly. Once again, and just like in the old days with Massimo, Francesca had found a way around the laborious obstacle of study and the rigors of examination. This time her ex-husband had nothing at all to do with her delirium of omnipotence.

Elena absolutely did not share Francesca's opinion that a university degree was of no good use, much less did she accept the idea when it had to do with a matter so delicate as psychology. If this was how things really stood, then she really did not know what to think about Marco as a professional. Was he trying so hard to gratify Francesca so as not to risk losing her?

But she said nothing, and Francesca, caught up as she was in her enthusiasm for the positive interest which she thought that she had raised in her cousin, did not notice Elena's silence.

Here it was again, that old arrogant disregard she had for the commitment to their university studies which she and Renato had dedicated when Francesca, at a very young age, had decided to marry Massimo and to ignore any possibility of economic independence from him. And now the situation was the same. In fact, it was much more serious, because this man was also deluding her that she could practice as a professional. This man, too, what game was he playing with Francesca's mind? But her efforts at understanding, at least for that morning, stopped there. She had to leave soon, but not before a second cup of coffee, the one that Francesca had made before Marco had left them to their conversation.

"So, let's talk on Friday evening and on Saturday, let's go to the open-air market and to the Outlets" were Francesca's last words as they stood at the door saying their farewells.

"Say goodbye to your Prince Charming for me," said Elena, re-using the words which before her visit, Francesca had used on the phone to describe him. "You were right, I think that he has charmed your senses and your intellect. 'Til Friday evening, then."

In fact, he had not reappeared, not even to say goodbye.

It had started to rain. The sun had not won out, and the monotonous rhythm of the wipers did nothing to clear Elena's mind crowded with a thousand thoughts.

In the two hours that they had spent chatting, Elena and

Francesca had certainly not managed to fill in the hole left by ten years of separation. For example, the occasion had not presented itself to ask what had pre-empted the separation from Massimo, but her allusion to him being tired of his wife's creativity and of her 'spending and squandering' was perhaps only the tip of the iceberg. Perhaps Renato was right about the importance of money in their relationship, and especially about the end of it.

Whatever had been the reason, the fact that Francesca had been 'charmed' by someone else must certainly have depended on an on-going crisis. Renato had summed it up in a few words and typically from a man's point of view, which concentrates on objective facts, such as the sudden lack of money and its consequent fall in the standard of living, without delving at all deeply.

Elena's musings stopped only when she had arrived at her appointment, but not before she had realized how happy she was to have found Francesca again. She was willing to not dig up old history, especially given that Francesca, liquidating the issue in a few words, had clearly indicated that she didn't want to go there. And anyway, she told herself, it would be of no use, since surely the root of those problems — that is, Massimo — was no longer in the picture. He had been the real Charmer then; her cousin's mind-bender for so many years, and no credit to Francesca because she had let him do it. And all those flights of fancy about education and careers — could those be left over from his brainwashing? Certainly Marco was flattering her a good deal, but given his profession, maybe he knew what he was doing ….

Too right he knew what he was doing.

Saturday's excursion was not the only time that they went out together, and within a couple of months, it seemed that they had once again found their old harmony. They saw each other more and more often, usually meeting up at Francesca's house, where Marco hardly ever put in an appearance, even though he was at home.

"Where's Marco?" Elena would ask.

"He's downstairs, busy with one of his therapy sessions," was Francesca's usual reply. But Elena soon started to feel that there was something odd about his continual absence from the scene. She began to suspect that he was not happy to see her so often, also because she could not forget that sensation she had felt when they had looked at each other for the first time, shaking hands, that she again perceived each time they had met.

There was something in those shifty eyes that avoided hers every time they spoke to each other. In fact, it happened every time that Elena or Francesca included him in their conversation, because he seemed to only want to be there as an observer. Could it be a professional inclination?

And then there was the way he held Francesca's hand the whole time, always, on those rare occasions when he sat down with the two of them in the kitchen or in the living room ...

It seemed to her that this ostentatious show of his love was excessive, and she had reached the point of thinking that, with this his behavior, he wanted to exclude her from their ideal world and to also demonstrate how different their relationship as a couple was from Francesca's previous one — one which Elena knew well.

And those strange hisses on the phone — the ones that she heard only when she was speaking to Francesca on the landline — was he spying on her? Was it that he wanted to be sure that Francesca was really going out with her? To be sure, not once had Marco stopped remarking on the fact that since Francesca had 'found' her cousin again, that she had also 'found' a way to kill time during the empty hours when he was busy with his patients. She went out; something that she had never done before.

He said this not with the contented tone of someone who feels relieved of a sense of guilt (even if it was only due to the exigencies of work) and was glad that his partner would not be bored waiting for him. No, there was a subtle irony in his voice which Francesca did not seem to perceive but which Elena did not miss. Like she also did not miss the sly way in which he unfailingly reminded Francesca of the preparation for the next session of the group, by coming out quickly with a "I want to see you shine like you always do in front of those eight pairs of admiring eyes," followed by, "have a nice walk, my Love. Have fun!" Not even a greeting to Elena, except for a hasty "bye".

Francesca defined all of this as an expression of Marco's pre-occupation with her being a success, and as an expression of how much he would miss her while she was away.

"Now, can you credit that? He can't go without me for even a minute. He's crazy in love with me and I find it so exhilarating."

Elena was more and more perplexed. She soon started to notice the soft-focus lens of tenderness through which Francesca perceived every statement and every gesture of her companion, managing in this way to pardon even his bad manners. For example, when he answered the phone and passed it to Francesca without even greeting Elena, saying rudely and making sure that Elena would hear him: "It's Elena again". Francesca would take the call and quickly say "Marco is so brusque because he doesn't want to take any time away from my conversation with you."

The first few times, Elena thought that Francesca would have done better to have kept her remark to herself, since she obviously didn't want to recognize the fact as pure ill-breeding. But then she understood that her cousin had acted in good faith and that what wasn't functioning was her ability to discern and interpret reality. So she didn't feel like telling her how irritating she found Marco's tone of voice when he said, "it's her," when passing the phone without even a greeting.

Elena began to piece together all the tiles of that ugly mosaic, starting from his handshake at their first meeting, when the fleeting contact of his hand had not been warm but as distasteful as were his eyes.

She knew quite a lot about body language, partly because she read a lot but largely because she was perceptive enough to border on being sensitive. So when she revisited that first negative feeling he had given her, she had needed to rationalize it with the fact — as she told herself again and again — that at least he made Francesca happy and that this was the only thing that really mattered. And anyway, even though she didn't completely agree with the negative opinion that Renato had of their cousin, she had begun to consider his viewpoint more and more, and to tell herself that maybe what he said was true and that something in this woman was not quite right.

It was with this in mind, and in order to get to know Marco better, and perhaps in order to dispel some of the doubts that she had about him, that she decided to invite them to lunch one Sunday, taking care to invite another couple who were also their friends, so as to create an informal and pleasant atmosphere. She would ensure that Marco would not feel himself to be the subject of an inquisition, and that she would not be reduced by him to the role of cook and waitress while he spent all his time flattering and petting his dear Francesca.

Unfortunately, everything went according to her worst predictions, in spite of the dampers she had put in place and all the effort she had dedicated to keeping the encounter lighthearted. It happened that, without intending to, she had unmasked his diabolical plan against Francesca.

In the most obvious way, Marco focused his conversation and his gaze only on Francesca and on the other two guests, never once speaking to Elena unless it was to fill her glass when he was pouring the wine for everyone.

Francesca did not seem to notice anything at all, and was unusually loquacious — something that Elena had never known her to be, with the exception of that horrible last day on the sailboat all those years ago, when she had gone on and on as though she were Massimo's trained parrot.

She spoke knowledgeably about a case that they had been discussing for some time. It was about the repeatedly self-destructive behavior which the daughter of the other couple seemed to adopt in every one of her love affairs.

In fact, as often happens when an expert in one thing or another is present, the other couple had asked Marco his opinion about it. He did express something, but he left Francesca plenty of room to discourse on complexes, pathologies and therapies while he sat there nodding his head in approval at her every word and tossing in a couple of times how she had got to the heart of the problem.

He even said that by now she had completely joined the ranks of his profession and that her collaboration was invaluable in the self-help group that they ran together.

At this, Elena could not help but wonder if she was not seated at table with another skillful Trainer of Parrots, and it didn't take long to answer that question.

In fact, they were on the main course in the middle of the meal when Francesca suddenly excused herself from the table, apologizing for having to interrupt the very interesting topic of conversation. It was at that point — that is, just after Francesca had left the room — that Marco made a very strange remark about how easy it is — once the weak point in anyone's personality has been identified — to use that knowledge as a lever to get what you want from that person.

The lightness of his tone and the way in which his words followed on from what one of us had just said earlier left no doubt as to the consequence of Marco's thoughts, but the other couple did not grasp the gravity of his words. It did not escape Elena, however, that it had been his private mental reference to Francesca, who had left the table with the sincere regret of a Grand Master in the middle of her great Dissertation.

Elena pretended to be indifferent and non-judgmental, because she did not want to block Marco from externalizing his thoughts, but Francesca was returning to the table and the conversation took up its previous line.

That day Elena understood the danger which Francesca was courting: a second subjugation and its consequent new alienation from reality.

Was it possible, she asked herself, that Francesca was so

weak-willed that she would become dependent on any manipulator who chose to subordinate her? Her current man was a professional in the field of mental control, but even Massimo had managed it without any special education.

She remembered that she had suspected this once before. It had been during the two group sessions which she had attended after joining their group the month before.

The deference with which Marco treated Francesca during the sessions had seemed excessive to Elena — almost servile — when he praised her observations and invited the participants to read the books from which she quoted during the sessions. It was as bad as his always holding her hand when the three of them were together.

But Elena hadn't given it much thought at that time, having already been told by Francesca about how much he admired Francesca's intellectual abilities.

"He admires me for my mind as well as for the body and the looks which Massimo was crazy about. My physical aspect is really important for Marco, too, and, of course, I couldn't stand not to be noticed, but now I finally feel whole and complete." She had come out with this one day when they were in the car after it had been mentioned that Massimo had conquered her and kept his hold on her by making her feel admired for her mind, which made her feel that she held sway over him.

"Body … brain … but what about soul?" Elena reflected. Did her cousin have a soul? Was she at all aware of her own self, besides or beyond what others thought she was? What did Francesca see when she looked in the mirror? Was it simply a beautiful empty shell? Or was it full of all those creepy syndromes that she was always dribbling out (and in which she had never taken any interest back when she was into Vogue magazine and those other glossies).

"Really? How is it that you came to be so interested in psychology?" she had asked Francesca on that occasion. "I mean, it seems to be such an integral part of you now…"

"Well, you know, I was searching for something to help me to not think about how life with Massimo had changed for the worse. Before, I used to go shopping or I would change the furnishings any way I liked without worrying about the cost, and then one day … that was it. Some friends of mine told me about some books and some New Age lectures and they got me to try out some different courses — you know, things like that dance course which is supposed to help your mind to express itself though movement — stuff like that. And then one day, when Massimo wanted to stay home on his own to sort out some bills, I took up a friend's invitation to try out a session on one of Marco's courses. End of story."

"Do you mean to say that you went straight into full immersion with psychology? What about Massimo? What did he think about it?" Elena had asked.

"What did he think about it? He was worried about the sessions costing too much. He never asked me anything about what we talked about in the group, until Marco managed to get us to all meet up and we started going out as a four-some. But all that happened a little while after we had met at dinner at the house of mutual friends. My friend's invitation to join the group session and the dinner invitation happened at around the same time and I only discovered later that it had been Marco who had told my friend to get me involved in the group because he'd noticed me at the dinner. Massimo and Marco's companion had both been there, you see."

There was that word again, between the two of them. Elena certainly did see … perfectly … and added more pieces to the puzzle of how Marco manipulated Francesca. Poor Massimo. He had had a role to play, too; designated from the very beginning to be written out of the scene, 'exit right' together with Marco's companion.

She found herself thinking about how ten years ago she had seen even Massimo fall prey to a much stronger character. She was reminded about his process of identification with Carlo that she had witnessed during just two days on the sailboat. Unlike what was happening now between Francesca and Marco, that hadn't been intentional on the part of Carlo. Musing about that first day together in Portofino, she wondered "Is it possible that weak minds can be influenced so easily by their own craving for success and glory? or that emulating someone does somehow fulfill a yearning within them?"

Elena had always known that Massimo dearly loved the sea and that he particularly loved to sail. Even when he was a boy, he had vowed to get his ship's passport one day, and that sooner or later he would buy a sailboat.

But, given his usual lack of tenacity in carrying out his projects, the seaman's license had only arrived long afterwards, a short while before the infamous sailing trip, when his fortune had dwindled to nearly nothing. Elena remembered Massimo and Francesca talking about going away on the weekends to look at sailboats, about the Salone Nautico in Genoa, about how Massimo felt as trapped as a caged lion because he couldn't make his dream of buying a sailboat come true as soon as the license was in his hand. The two of them had even said that the sailboat would materialize once Francesca had received her part of an inheritance and that she had already been summoned by the lawyer about it.

That was why Elena had suggested to Carlo to invite them along to Sardinia that summer — the summer that was the end of their friendship.

"Darling, you should see how his eyes light up each time I tell my cousin and her husband about us sailing on Sundays. Massimo's always wanted a sailboat — it's his heart's desire. But he's always put Francesca's wishes first, and his pocket is pretty stretched right now. Would you like to get to know them and invite them out with us one Sunday? Actually, if you agree, I would love to take them with us on our sail to Sardinia. Although, it is a fact that they have never lived on board before so I don't know if it is really the case … especially Francesca. I don't really see her adapting (what with her ideas about comfort, which is of zero interest to her). If it gets in the way of her striking an impression, she is willing to throw practicality and convenience out of the window."

"On the whole, I can't say that I'm all that enthusiastic about the idea, and I have to admit that I wouldn't want to find myself stuck with two fish out of water. But if you really want to, why not? Let's invite them to go out on the water with us these next few Sundays before the trip and we'll see how it goes" Carlo had replied, as willing as Elena had expected him to be.

Massimo was in Seventh Heaven when she phoned him, and he didn't waste a minute. It was on a Friday — Elena remembered it well — and he had said that they would kit themselves out the very next day with the bare necessities and that Francesca was sure to agree.

But on Sunday morning, Massimo had appeared alone at the port, saying that Francesca sent her apologies because she had not managed to get herself ready in time for the sail. Later that evening, when Massimo had gone home, Carlo had asked Elena what could Francesca need besides a pair of jeans and a windbreaker?

"My cousin is like that" was her lighthearted reply and they spoke no more about it.

"On the other hand," Carlo had continued "Massimo seems to me to be very enthusiastic and capable — maybe a little overdressed in designer clothes for my taste, but that's his business."

So the two men had got to know each other and they had clicked as fellow sailors. Elena was glad for Massimo. As for Francesca, knowing her well, she would go along with Massimo and his nautical fancies, even if she had never professed any great love for the sea.

Carlo knew that Elena was very fond of those two, because she spoke often of them. He also knew all about the rather platonic little love story that there had been between Elena and Massimo when she was twenty. He knew that she saw them often and that the three of them had practically become a little family. So, given that the chance for him to join them had not yet come up, he was delighted with Elena's suggestion.

Notwithstanding the fact that Elena had always said that she was very different from them and from their way of seeing things, Carlo had never been biased against the two of the them. The fact that she was so fond of them, no matter what, made him appreciate her all the more.

"One thing that I like about you" he had said "is your ability to glide over diversity. You do it so well that you could get palm trees to grow at the North Pole."

As a matter of fact, he wasn't wrong when it came to her cousin and her husband. Even though Elena was the last person who he could ever imagine as being so full of arrogance as to consider herself superior to everyone and everything, that sort of attitude certainly did pertain to that pair, whom he had not yet met. He had come to know through Elena that they were good-for-nothings with little beyond a riding stable which Massimo did not know how to run, and that they had allowed themselves to not bother to finish university or to get a job. From what she said, the two of them were cast from the same mold, but he had never pre-judged anyone over their choice of lifestyle. He himself had made his own way in life, as had Elena, and his motto had always been to let others do whatever they felt like doing.

He was firmly convinced that Elena was right when she had told him: "You know, when you grow up on a large family estate and you realize that you will inherit a large chunk of it, it can radically change your point of view when you are contemplating the goal of a university degree. Massimo started various degree courses, but pretty much in the same spirit as if he were choosing the optionals for his luxury cars or his motorcycles. And after he finally stopped pretending to be a student — which was not before getting Francesca enrolled together with him in some faculty or other that I can't even remember — he had enough money to allow himself to invest a good deal of capital in the stables which I told you about. It's just that, if we are talking about his interest in horses, I have no doubt that he is interested in them, because we had always seen him on horseback and we all knew how much he loved his first horse, the one he still had when he met Francesca…"

"And who is 'we all'?" interrupted Carlo, who was more curious than ever about this absurd story which was so far removed from everyday life.

"Everyone in our circle of friends. Even when we were in high school, the kids at university kept in touch with us younger ones. Not Francesca though, because she was practically still in diapers. Anyway, I was telling you that it was one thing for him to love his animals and it was another thing altogether his ability to administer an amount of capital invested too heavily in unsteady variables — like animals, which eat a lot and have to be looked after, and like the weather, which influences the number of your customers. And this is without taking into account that Massimo has never had to rise early to tackle the day, or whatever," said Elena.

"When he was boy, unless it was raining, Massimo went out riding every afternoon on his handsome purebred stallion, which looked as aristocratic as his owner. He didn't only ride over his family's land, which was just outside the city limits, but also along the connecting roads around it." Elena continued, "You'll see for yourself what a distinguished air Massimo has about him, like someone from another époque: tall, slim, and with what used to be jet black hair but is now greying a bit at the temples. And when he was young, he had a look about him of an English Gentleman, as though he had stepped out of an engraving of a fox hunt, if you know what I mean. He used to say that he loved horses because by their nature, they were high class, and by their pace, they were dignified. To say it all in a single word: for their *elegance*. And we would maliciously mutter under our breath 'For your arrogance,' each and every time he said it. But we all liked him anyway."

"And you were even in love with him," said Carlo.

"It's true." said Elena "But I was only twenty and he was

older than me and he was the only one I could talk to for hours on end about books, so I took the shadow for the substance. Certainly there is no way that it could happen now — we are way too different."

"Tell me about the riding stable," said Carlo.

"The stable … it lasted for a few years, but it was creaking in every joint despite appearances. As you can imagine from everything that I've told you about the owner, it was a very exclusive sports center where even the stable boys had to treat the clientele with exquisite manners. And the customers were the very cream of high society, some even coming from as far away as other cities. It was the best Country Club among all the local ones and it was there that Francesca arrived one day, a fresh-faced eighteen-year-old on the heels of one of her brothers. He was away at university in Switzerland but looking for a place where he could ride when he was back in Italy for the holidays. Massimo was dazzled by that beauty "not yet in full bloom" as he described it to me years later. Or perhaps it was simply that she didn't show off yet, so hers was a loveliness that was muted by the painful shyness of a tall, blonde, Nordic-looking girl. When we were talking about it, he confided that he had immediately dubbed her 'Ingrid' in his mind — Bergman, of course. And that was the name that he always called her by for the next ten years or more, that is, when we hung out together," said Elena.

"So she practically bewitched him at first sight" said Carlo.

"You're right, it was just like that, but his getting her to understand to what degree … that was his downfall."

"But Elena, don't you think that you're exaggerating? It's like you want to excuse him for having ruined his own life with his own hands — at least that's what I have managed to understand about the character you have described."

"No, absolutely not. And I know that it can be difficult to understand. The fact is that even that name (and he called her that not just in private when they were alone but also in public) helped her wipe out of her mind even the tiniest residue of insecurity, and that contributed to her becoming the monster of effrontery which she is today with him, in giving all her pretensions a foundation. I told you that he can no longer afford a sailboat — well, if he had been a bit more prudent and a bit less ready to make his Ingrid's every wish come true, then he could have bought three boats. Anyway, I'm telling you all this just because I can confide in you and I want you to know something about the people we are going to be sailing with. And I say it with all the affection which I feel for them. Otherwise I would never have suggested taking them with us to Sardinia, you know?"

"Of course, I understand. Don't worry, I don't think that you are just gossiping," Carlo assured her. "But did they really have such a high standard of living that they ran through an entire fortune, which, from what you are saying, must have been considerable?"

"Exactly that. They were profligate in their spending, especially him, who was the more mature, as they say, of the two. I'll say it again that she was and still is just a doll caught up in his flattery and pampering, so much so that he's put it into her head that it's enough for her to bat her beautiful eyelashes to get whatever she wants in life."

"Listen, I can't wait to meet them. I'm really curious now and …" said Carlo.

"And what?" asked Elena.

"And God help us, because I don't think that she's the sailing type. I mean someone who can deal with the spartan living conditions on board. It's definitely not the same as being on a luxury cruise with the Crociere Costa company," said Carlo.

"You've hit the nail on the head. That's why I want them to set out with us these next couple of Sundays before we sail, and let them help get the ship ready. That will give you the chance to study them," said Elena.

And that was how Carlo and Massimo checked the ship inside and out over the next two weeks, becoming old friends and old tars, going to lunch together at the restaurant in the shipyard where Carlo kept his boat, and returning home late at night content, both of them pleased as well with their new friendship. By that time, Carlo seemed to have discounted Francesca, since she seemed to be in a distinct minority, and would anyway have to adapt to the situation. No matter how spoiled she was, she was no longer a child.

The day for the sail arrived and the four of them had arranged to meet at the ship at around nine in the morning, even though Elena, Carlo, and Carlo's son would have been there much earlier. They were more experienced — even the boy was an expert sailor — and everything had to be perfect.

The day was very hot even at that early hour and Francesca was simply ridiculous when she appeared on the quay in her yachting outfit suitable for a luxury cruise, and came down the pier which separated the boats from the parking lot.

It was obvious that in her mind those twenty meters of the pier had been transformed into the catwalk of a fashion show. Perhaps she had even practiced for days beforehand how to do her promenade. And from the other boats, everyone — literally everybody — had turned around to watch her, placing their hands above their eyes to shade them from the hot August sun above.

She was stunning, but she stuck out like a sore thumb compared with the others in their comfortable clothes. These were people who were used to living on the waves and not according to the glossy fashion magazines which she, instead, must have studied hard during those preparatory days. And the clothes must have made her feel quite hot as well.

Elena knew that her cousin had always declared herself to be 'athermic', when her being "heat-proof" was a way to justify there not being a single blouse or dress in her wardrobe that did not have long sleeves — not even among the summer clothes. But that day, she had really gone overboard, appearing in a navy double-breasted blazer with gold buttons, white trousers and leather lace-ups with leather soles. In their bermuda shorts and espadrilles, Elena and the other women along the wharf looked like cabin boys ready to sail and to lade the Princess's sea trunks on the yacht anchored nearby.

It knocked Carlo's breath right out of him … for the simple reason that he immediately realized that he had to stop Francesca from coming on board with those shoes. He managed to find the right words and the diplomatic incident ended there. She hadn't even noticed the embarrassment she had caused, taken as she was with her role of 'prima donna'.

While they were taking their elegant luggage on board, Elena wondered how it was that Massimo had not noticed how out of place his wife had appeared, but even this thought had not lasted long because Francesca had changed into more comfortable clothes, and they had all set to work. Even Antonio, who had the job of storing the bottles of mineral water in a safe corner where they would stay cool.

But there were other surprises to come in the next few hours before they were due to set sail in the early afternoon.

The two men started tinkering with the engine, which Carlo had stopped working on when the other couple had arrived. Observing them in action, Elena noticed that Massimo was wearing very practical clothing, although it was always in that refined style of his and with the colors well-matched. This was the first time — and she had known him for a long time — she had ever seen him wearing a T-shirt and not one of the tailor-made shirts he always dressed in whether it be winter or summer. Even when on horseback, he was well-known for his riding coats and safari jackets.

But Elena only realized this after a while. What had really caught her attention was the assured way he moved on deck — conferring with Carlo, but as though he knew the ship inside out and had already clocked up hours and hours of sailing.

That tall dark man whom she thought she had always known so well, and who had fascinated her so many years ago, suddenly appeared to her a stranger. She put it down to his elation at finding himself in his element — the sea — with the woman he loved, and the happy prospect of a two-week sail.

His rather haughty way of seeming to look down on everyone from a pedestal had disappeared, and he appeared to be comfortable even with Antonio, whom he had only just met for the first time. So much so that the boy had immediately taken to him without being awed.

In jeans and a T-shirt, he seemed absolutely 'ordinary' and, for the first time, it was Francesca who was the one who seemed to clash by his side. She looked as though she were there by mere chance, on her way to some social event ashore. This was even after she had changed into a pair of shorts and a matching top, that emphasized the long legs and shapely bust that Massimo's long years of compliments had taught her to flaunt. It would have been perfect at dinner time, but not for helping Elena to organize the galley and stow the cabin. Fortunately, she was full of good will.

Massimo even spoke in a different way, but Elena couldn't manage to stop the tape of that incredible film in order to see what had caused the metamorphosis.

Finding herself near Francesca, Elena asked quietly so that the other two could not overhear: "What's up with Massimo today? He seems different."

"He's been like this for a week" replied Francesca "ever since the last time that you went to lunch together here and then went out for a sail, while I was at the Outlets."

"And…?" Elena encouraged her.

"And that's all. He's done nothing else but say over and over again that Carlo is a great guy, that Carlo is that best friend that he's always wanted, that Carlo is the Perfect Man that he's never found before… He likes the casual way that Carlo dresses. And isn't Carlo lucky to have a good income, a sailing ship, and … a son," Francesca reported.

"Did he open that old wound again?" asked Elena.

"Yes. But who the hell cares? He'll get over it — two weeks on the water will take his mind off that obsession. Really, can you believe that we still have to talk about it? We agreed at the very beginning — even you know we did!" Francesca replied.

Elena dropped the subject, and Francesca knew how to read that diplomatic silence.

Antonio interrupted them with an enterprising idea for the trip they were about to begin: "How about getting some nets ready to cast for squid? There will be hundreds of them all around the boat tonight. No spear guns, though, because we'll want to throw them back."

"Oh, of course," agreed Elena. "Meanwhile go ahead and get yours ready. I put it on that seat just two minutes ago."

Antonio had been thinking about squid while dragging the case of bottled water, and it was because he had dropped it just behind Elena in order to reach for the net that Elena had tripped over the case and had fallen onto the table and onto the bread-knife. After that everything turned rather topsy-turvy and surreal, tragically ending for Elena her lifelong friendship with her cousin. And, although she had never wanted to face it before, there was the proof of the mental lability of Francesca and Massimo.

Massimo, though, was the one who remained fixed in her mind for the next ten years as the driving force, albeit some-times weak, behind everything that had happened.

Elena thought about all of this in those ten minutes that Francesca, at her house, was away from the table, and while Marco made his assertions on the weaknesses of other people.

So that was why he paid such excessive attention to her cousin's intellectual abilities ... and the reason why he rec-ommended all that reading to her, and which she so proudly mentioned in their friendly conversations.

Francesca even told her that up until the time that the two of them had started seeing each other again, that she would usually spend her time reading and preparing for the weekly group-therapy session while Marco was working. Not that she had stopped doing so now, but that before, she had never gone out without him — ever.

The meal was over, but the five friends lingered over coffee and the chocolates that Francesca had brought along, before saying their farewells in the late afternoon.

Later, while she was clearing up the kitchen and straightening the living room, Elena went over in her mind the many small details that she had noticed in the last few months — particulars that she had not really paid much attention to before, because she had seen things through the ardent eyes of Francesca, who was living a totally new relationship after the routine of a twenty-year marriage.

But after what had happened during the lunch, the puzzle seemed to make more sense, though she did not at all like the picture that had emerged.

She decided that that man must have a plan in mind, and it wasn't limited to just keeping hold of that precious gem that he had acquired… Or better said, that the reason for his not wanting to lose her was not simply his being madly in love with Francesca, as he would have liked everyone, not only her, to believe.

And that the very obvious antipathy which he felt for her — Elena — could not merely be the dislike which everyone, sooner or later, feels for some other person.

The more she thought about it, the more she was convinced that Marco, no matter how odd and peculiar he was, must anyway know the basics of good manners in order to deal with people. He could not have practiced his profession without knowing how to establish a rapport with his patients, nor especially how to be sociable, even if he did not socialize much in his private life.

No, what he felt about her was not simply a strong instinctive dislike — it was pure hate, which enveloped him whenever she and Francesca were together and whether or not other people were present. And it was a strong emotion which he could not manage to control, even if he was a professional in that area. It had to be connected to something which she could not yet put her finger on… But at some point, he would give himself away again, just as he had during Francesca's brief absence from the table. Yes, that must be the way to disentangle the muddle: if seeing Francesca and her together set off a reaction of uncontrollable hatred, then finding himself alone with her had made him drop his guard and he had let loose that affirmation about weak points that can be manipulated.

The Great Specialist that Francesca bragged about was not able to control himself nor to relate to common situations in which it would be enough to follow common sense. Not only should his professional position have kept him from revealing his ability to manipulate others — especially during an informal conversation and outside the confines of a medical setting — but his expertise should have given him the lucidity to control his own feelings.

Something was not right in that man: something pathological or something diabolical. And Elena intended to understand it and to unmask it if this were essential for the good of Francesca.

Truly rude or not, she had deduced that the special treatment he reserved for her alone could only be part of a well-conceived plan to keep an enemy at a good distance. And considering that he was well competent in psychology, this must be a tactic he had used before with success. But, why?

Even during the group-therapy session, she reflected, he had never once spoken to her, nor had he called the others' attention to what she was saying. And if any of the other participants had commented on her thoughts, he had always quickly intervened by saying "Quite true; I hadn't noticed" but without ever adding the "sorry" which instead he always directed to the others in the exceedingly rare instances that this had happened.

Could it be mere coincidence?

"No. This is "the thread by which hangs the tale ..." she said to herself, repeating the phrase as she stood before the refrigerator door, about to put away a platter of leftovers from a dish that Marco had offered to everyone except her.

He was treating her as though she were not there — see-through, non-existent — exactly the same as in an article she had read on psychiatric medicine. This was the way that some patients 'related' to the world, that is, they isolated themselves from it. And their isolation induced many people to distance themselves from those patients and to set them adrift, so that it is only the people who care about them who insist on maintaining a relationship with them, despite their evasive behavior.

It seemed obvious to her that a psychiatrist had to know how this way of behaving, even beyond any pathological situation, would affect the life of an ordinary person. No one likes to feel rejected and, according to Marco, sooner or later she would be driven away.

What was this Mastermind afraid of? What was his underhanded aim which he feared Elena might ruin? Because at table, when he had talked about vulnerable personalities, about weak points, the person he had in mind was certainly Francesca.

She would not give up; she would get to the bottom of this and verify her sudden striking insight that her cousin had fallen out of the pan and into the fire.

A few days went by and one morning, when Elena went to Francesca's house, she found her in the upstairs living room surrounded by books and scientific dictionaries dispersed around the sofa and on armchairs.

"Come on in. Just move a few books out of the way and sit down," she said. "I'm a little behind in preparing for today's session. You're coming, aren't you?"

"Sure I am," replied Elena. "I just stopped by for that coffee you invited me for yesterday when we spoke on the phone. I'll come back later at six o'clock."

"Great. I really do need a break. Come on, let's move into the kitchen. But I really can't stop for more than a coffee — sorry! — because I want to give a lesson that is on the same high level as Marco."

"A lesson? Won't it be an open talk, like it usually is?"

"Yes, of course. It's just that the main theme that we've chosen is so serious and so stimulating, that — you'll see — I will have a lot of things to say against those pigs. The subject this evening is about pedophilia. The idea came to mind as we were watching the news on television, that terrible case of the uncle who had abused his nine-year-old niece and then he justified himself by saying that she had consented. Did you hear about it?"

"Of course I heard about it. Horrifying."

"When we talked about it, Marco said that these things do exist, and society has to face it and treat pedophiles without passing judgement on them … and nothing more. I think that's too little and I want to be well prepared, even ready to rebut him, if necessary. Don't you think I'm right? He is so detached … professionally, I mean. Not me. I go off my head when I hear about these things."

"You're right. I would lock them up for life and throw away the key. As much treatment as you like, but keep them away from any possible innocent little victims."

If Francesca had managed to have an idea of her own, and a strong one at that, then perhaps she really was growing up, thought Elena as she finished her coffee. But the conversation stopped there. They confirmed their meeting for later that evening and exchanged their usual affectionate goodbyes.

Something strange was brewing when Elena returned that evening. She was ten minutes late, which was unusual for her. Strangely, everyone was already there and Marco had already started the session. Was this another coincidence? Usually he conceded a quarter-of-an-hour's grace for attendance. Anyway, the discussion was still at the informal stage because, as soon as Marco and Francesca had informed them of the topic the two of them had chosen, everyone had immediately formed small sub-groups and these, for the moment, were only producing a lot of buzzing. And then Elena realized that the reason for the upset was that the usual order of the day, which was that Francesca always spoke first, had been changed.

Evidently this was something new for the others as well. Certainly, ever since Elena had joined the group, Marco had always invited Francesca to take the floor first, with an overindulgent deference that only she seemed to have noted.

It took her nearly the entire first hour of the usual two-hour session for Elena to realize why Marco had wanted today's change. From the way that the debate had immediately taken shape, it seemed that everyone agreed that the news item reported by the media should be considered as shocking, and that this sort of thing seemed to be happening more and more frequently.

Francesca's eyes expressed her unceasing approval, and her impatience to ratify this point of view about the news stories they all knew about, and which Marco had briefly summarized ... but why did he not let her speak? And why was there no praising of her?

A sudden thought flashed through her mind — something apparently irrelevant had happened that morning when she and Francesca were talking about the upcoming session. Elena had needed something from her handbag which she had left at the door and she had gone out of the kitchen to go and fetch it. She had nearly bumped into Marco, who was standing in front of the console table looking for something, but the table had been completely bare except for the lamp. Only now had she realized the obvious: that he had been there spying on the preparatory work for that evening's session. Francesca had already made it clear to him that, for once, her stance would not agree with his and the general consensus would surely agree with her, if only because it was the most common opinion on the topic. Marco had to maintain control over the other minds, which instead, and just as the opening debate seemed to be demonstrating, would concur with Francesca.

Marco began to comment on the facts in a way diametrically opposed to what the others would have expected, including Francesca, who, when she had been speaking with Elena earlier, had interpreted his cynicism as being purely a professional detachment from the subject.

It took no more than a couple of minutes for the group, including Francesca, to fall silent and to hang on his every word, slightly incredulous at first, but later completely subjugated as they listened to the words of the Great Guru.

This was certainly not what Elena would have expected after Francesca's brief but passionate speech this morning. But what most made her indignant and what intrigued her was the sudden lack of reaction from those present. There was not even a simple discomfited shift of a body in a chair, nor was anyone raising a hand for permission to comment.

In a rising tide of banalities and nonsense, Marco was asserting that pedophilia existed, that it was a 'behavior' to be battled, obviously, but that it was to treated like all illnesses and not punished; that it couldn't be marginalized because it was as old as the hills ... and then it all culminated with his decisive declaration that, more often than it was commonly believed, it was the children themselves who provoked the emergence of this disturbance which is latent in adults.

Where was he going with this? Was it possible that it was simply his need for power that had induced him to this point? In what brute's hands and bed had Francesca ended up?

All these questions crowded into Elena's mind and, as she noted the passive attitudes of the others, she fathomed how Marco was channeling the message of his command over their minds and was reassuming his precedence over his much fawned-upon companion when it came to expressing concepts. It made Elena leap to her feet and blurt out, "How can you make such a filthy statement?!"

In total silence, Marco recalled her to order, extending an arm in her direction with an arrogant gesture to peremptorily block whatever she was about to say.

No one drew a breath — not even Francesca. They had acknowledged The Truth.

As for Francesca's lesson, there had not been even a glimpse. On the contrary, she had nodded her head at every statement he had made. Elena had now seen it confirmed that the slow reawakening of her cousin, which had been due to their exchange of ideas, had been identified and suppressed at birth. That was why Marco had wanted at any price to drive her away.

The Great Leader declared the debate open and the first of those present to have raised his hand, a professional man well into his fifties, actually said that he fully agreed that children contributed to these things happening every day. He supported his argument with an assertion about the age of the little girl who was involved in this incident that had been reported by the media: nine years old, that is, two years over the age of reason. With her provocative behavior, it had been the girl who had awoken the sexual interest of the thirty-year-old uncle.

Elena was appalled and responded that what he described as 'provocative behavior' in any nine-year-old child was nothing more than the product of the surroundings in which she lived, including the media.

Her debater laconically answered, "If I as an adult warn her, explaining that I might hurt her a lot, and she insists, well, my conscience is clear and I can proceed."

Elena looked first at Francesca, as though to give her a push to introduce the arguments she had prepared. Silence. Then she turned her eyes elsewhere, running around the circle from Marco to the other seven. Nothing. So, in a voice so calm that it sounded almost resigned, she said: "Don't you think that we should mention the moral principles — or call it ethics for those delicate ears of the laity — which are in force for any event in life? And taboos? I'm pretty sure that sex with children is taboo."

It was only after a long two-minute silence that another group member took the floor, but it was only to say with some rancor, "Why must you always be Miss Contrary?"

There was not a trace of rebuke from Marco, who should, as he habitually did, have reminded the member who had spoken that the first rule of a group like theirs was to respect any other opinion without direct personal attacks on whoever had expressed it.

The Charmer really had worked with alacrity to control and subjugate his acolytes, thought Elena, asking herself how much pathological self-gratification of his ego there was in his actions and how much economic interest. Perhaps this had something to do with Francesca as well … and that reminded her about her uncle's Will which was still tied up, and Francesca's inheritance which Massimo had also been counting on.

The second theme of the session was taken up; something much less absorbing, for which Marco, with his usual mellifluous air, offered the floor to Francesca, who was pleased all the same. Equilibrium had been re-established. But not for Elena, who now had hands-on proof of how the situation was weighed against Francesca and who had just been illuminated as to the financial swindle which Marco surely had in mind.

Within the next couple of weeks, Elena very tactfully withdrew from the therapy group, without ever having talked about what had happened with Francesca, who might have been ashamed. (Elena was not entirely sure that Francesca had enough of a conscience for that.) She invented the excuse that her hours of work had changed and she could not help but note the sigh of relief from everyone. But, maintaining the consistency of character for which she was well known, she did not add that she was sorry, because that was not the case.

It was her intention to not make a public enemy of Marco and to not expose her flank so that he could eliminate her from Francesca's life.

Francesca had swallowed the lie; he hadn't. Yet it was to his advantage to keep quiet about it. If he were to provoke Elena into a verbal reaction in front of the group, then she, with a parting shot, would certainly at the very least have shaken that house of cards that he had carefully constructed, first of all for Francesca to see and then for the others, who paid handsomely for the weekly sessions that made them all feel part of a strong pack. Because they had all been tamed by an expert manipulator of brains and of unhappy souls. For Marco, Elena's dues were not an important loss.

Only now was she able to understand how it was that at Elena's first group-therapy session one of the girls in the group, when introducing herself (as each of the group did to the new arrival), had made such a point of informing her that thanks to the strength which Marco had given her, she had managed to walk over hot coals without burning herself.

As she said this, she had looked at her Holy Man with the languid and adoring eyes of someone enamored. It was obvious that he had convinced her that she had performed the feat. In Elena's opinion, what was supposed to be a group dedicated to self-analysis and self-consciousness had instead transformed itself into a veritable sect dedicated to its Great Priest. She told herself that she would not have been at all surprised to find out that all the women in the group would have voluntarily offered him their bodies without any jealousy, just so that they could belong completely to him.

That was not what Elena had been looking for when she had joined the group, tempted by Francesca's description of the "positive energy that the group created during session" and of Marco's ability to intuit and socialize. Now she told herself over and over again that she had made a big mistake when she had accepted him on trust only because (according to her) he had to have been better than Massimo.

At that point though, she began to seriously worry about Francesca's mental well-being, because she certainly had not knowingly placed herself in that slimy environment. How to get her out of there became Elena's greatest concern, and she asked herself how she could have not realized before how labile and dependent was her cousin's personality ... because unless it was so, how could this second mental surrender have happened? And the second subjugation was worse than the first.

Over the next few days, Elena's mind returned again and again to those two terrible days when ten years ago they had been on the boat with Massimo and Francesca. She remembered that even then she had wondered how a man who was so feeble (a victim himself of a process of identification with another man he admired and envied) could, in his own turn, be able to completely control another person's mind.

Her sudden insight, after a ten-year delay, led her to understand that there had been two different processes of identification, and she had to admit that Massimo had come out of it the winner. He had been so fascinated by Carlo that he imitated him, having idealized and envied him. Instead, Francesca conformed to whoever seemed to her to be able to offer her an excuse for all that was lacking in her existential state.

"Now I feel complete," Francesca kept saying, "as though I had always lived without a part of me that I did not know existed."

As for Massimo, she had never actually heard Francesca say so, but it was evident that for twenty long years the fictitious story had always been that it was only Massimo who could fill her emptiness — except that he then appeared to be totally useless to her, and was easily substituted as soon as his means were gone.

It was painful for Elena to admit that Francesca had behaved like a trained parrot for almost all her life, but she could not deny the evidence anymore. She had reached the point where she now viewed Francesca as the main cause for the ruin of her ex-husband — something which she had never wanted to admit before, not even with Renato.

When Massimo's process of identification with Carlo had evolved to the second stage — project planning — Francesca should have realized that he was going beyond the limit, rather than aping him in excluding Elena from the new circle of friends.

Elena understood that Francesca was completely lacking in scruples because she lacked a conscience which would impose operating limits ..., but was this not the same thing as saying that she was not intelligent?

As fond as she was of Francesca, Elena wanted to furnish her with an alibi no matter what.

And it was for the same motive that she continued to frequent the couple after the group-therapy episode which had ended so badly. She had decided to regain for her cousin her freedom of choice. But to do so she needed to know more about their life together, their daily routine and their love life.

What she was to discover would leave her speechless.

One afternoon the following winter, while they were speaking more openly than usual because Marco was away abroad at a conference, Francesca suddenly burst into tears and baldly stated that she was sure that Marco was seeing another woman.

Elena was not in the least surprised and asked her, "So why does he make such a big show about holding hands all the time? And the thing about exchanging looks, especially when you do it before you let yourself smile at anyone else?"

"Because that's the way he is. I've told you before that he charms people ... and then..."

"And then...?"

"And then it's that I'm firmly convinced that there are other things — things beyond sex — that he will never find in anyone else. He has such a high opinion of my mind... I'm sure that he would never leave me because he couldn't live without the stimulation and the intellectual fulfillment that I give him."

Out of pity, Elena gently skirted around Francesca's delusions, and although she would have liked to find out more, she did not push the issue that evening. She had discovered enough for the time being and she wanted Francesca to spontaneously open up to her. Also, they had already decided beforehand that Elena would stay over that night, since Marco wasn't home and Francesca did not want to be alone.

Elena promised herself again that she would think of some way to help Francesca to escape from the vortex in which she was trapped — a double tangle of convictions which were not only wrong but had also been imposed on her from an external source. She wanted her cousin to be convinced of Marco's dishonesty and, something even more painful, she wanted Francesca to see how she lacked any substance in his eyes, and how pointless she was in that universe of his, which was composed of futility and self-glorification.

But how could Elena tell her all this? How could she tell her that Francesca had unfortunately let herself be manipulated and contaminated by exactly that vanity?

The next morning, while they were still in their dressing gowns at the breakfast table, they returned to the conversation which they had left half-discussed the night before.

Francesca seemed to be back in full control of her emotions, as beautiful as ever and completely rested. She was wrapped in an unusual cape of light-blue cashmere which she said that she used as a robe and which she wore over the leggings and matching loose top that she used as pyjamas.

She had set the table with her usual flair and, since it was nearly Christmas, she had decorated it in her own style with dark plates and dark cups and dark napkins.

As though the conversation had never been interrupted, Francesca came out with "He could never give all this up."

"Listen," said Elena, "I've been thinking a lot about what you told me last night and I have to say that I did not expect to see you in such good form this morning. Just think: I listened at your door last night just in case you were crying. Obviously your ability to recover is fine — which is good. But, to my mind, you shouldn't rely on your feeling that he will never leave you because your relationship is founded on values that go beyond sex. Francesca, everything you said about values is sacrosanct, but is it truly enough for you that he doesn't leave you? Within a couple there is no substitute for physical intimacy and that is especially true if one or the other is looking outside the relationship for an alternative to what is missing, don't you think?"

"You are so right, and I can say that I know for sure that Marco is a monogamous man" replied Francesca.

"Great. But maybe it's that the two of you have not had sex for several months, is that it? I'm guessing here because you said that he's been seeing another woman but that he could never find anyone else who could maintain that intellectual understanding he has with you, right?"

"You've got it."

"So, don't you think that it could be that in keeping with his faithful nature that he is staying physically true to the other woman?"

"No, not that."

"But why not that? How can you be so sure?"

"Because there is no one else like me. He tells me that all the time."

"But you know how it is sometimes, we are all willing to sugar-coat the bitter pill a bit, aren't we? To tell a white lie, in other words."

"No, not him. Because he is too caught up by my brain. He told me that, too" said Francesca. "And anyway, you've seen for yourself how he puts me in charge of the group sessions and how everyone, including him, hangs on my every word."

She had completely identified herself with him. It would be impossible to shift her away from her mindset without being brutal: by throwing in her face the fact that it was absolutely not true, by reminding her about the session on pedophilia, and by daring to say that he kept her away from the real world and from the truth by making her believe that he had put her on a pedestal ... while instead what he really did was to keep her isolated in the ivory tower of his own mind — keeping her gathered together with his other trophies — and to who knows what end?

Elena could not imagine that the aim of all this was so frivolous and mean. It was too ridiculous to even consider that the Great Man wanted to avoid being alone for even one second while the baton passed between Francesca, shuttling out the door, and the new queen, installing herself in his domain. This is what it was all about: the Great Mind was afraid of solitude, just like any other poor devil.

"Okay. You do not want to listen to me and I, on the other hand, do not want you to think that I am just trying to break up your relationship," Elena said (though she should have added "just like you did to me ten years ago"). "Just promise me that you know that you can count on me and that you will confide in me whenever you need to, because, believe me, given your suspicions, you should be prepared for a nasty turn of events. And don't you think it's odd that he's had all these conferences in the last few months? And that they always seem to take place on holidays and over the weekends?"

"Well, why not? What's so strange about that? More than the fact that I trust him, I know that he would never do anything that would make him lose me."

"Alright. Didn't you say that he had one coming up over New Year's Eve? Excuse me, but it seems to me to be a pretty improbable date to ask people to be discussing their subject matter on the night of the thirty-first of December, and during the day on the first of January. And also, why is he not taking you with him?" And then she kept quiet as she waited for Francesca to reflect on her words, and for the effect of her words to hit ("should her brain still be capable of it" thought Elena).

After nearly a minute of silence, the expression on Francesca's face passed from one of arrogant self-assurance about what she was asserting to sobbing tears, her shoulders heaving as she sent the cups rattling, throwing her arms down heavily onto the table.

"What? Tell me!" said Elena, quickly grasping the chance when Francesca dropped her guard.

"I found some air tickets. They all have the right dates, but the destination ... the destination ... is different. It's always the same."

"And where is he going?"

"He's not going abroad, like he says he does. He always goes to Vicenza, where I know that one of his patients has moved. I know her, too. She used to come to him with her husband for marriage counseling."

"As far as professional behavior goes, that doesn't seem to me to be the most correct," Elena dryly remarked, and immediately regretted having said it, as it occurred to her that

Francesca had been Marco's patient, without even mentioning that his previous partner had been, too.

"Why not? What's so strange about that? After all, when it comes to love, anything can happen, right?"

"Exactly. Just as you say … when it comes to love. But not in his profession or, at least, not in that way … in a series." It was worth her while at this point for Elena to thrust the sword in up to the hilt because Francesca had just defended Marco, and because, in her self-serving delusion of power, Francesca had negated the evidence even to herself. And she would have kept doing so if Elena had forced her to keep talking rather than letting her decide to or not. Like a shipwrecked person, she had clung to the proffered lifeline, and she had done so well before the time that Elena had estimated that it would take.

Francesca now cried over her exploded myth, and for herself, because putting the whole situation into words had conferred on it a reality which she had always negated.

"Now calm down," said Elena. "There is a cure for everything, you know. You could make sure not to be home when he returns."

"I don't know where to go. I haven't got any kind of a job to maintain myself with nor a roof over my head."

"There is my house, if you want," reassured Elena, "and you can stay as long as you like. You can be certain of that. Now do tell me how you ever managed to play the part of the happy fulfilled woman with all of this churning around inside?"

"I don't know. Each time that I convinced myself that it was time to go — to leave him — he seemed to read my mind before we talked about it. Once he even accused me of thinking without first confiding in him … first, you see? And you tell me if it isn't love this need to get inside my head."

"Francesca, that isn't love. That is called 'brainwashing'. Look, we've got a couple of days to get things organized and after that, let's let him come home to an empty house."

"No. Because he will punish me from a distance."

"Now, let's not get carried away here. We never liked each other, he and I, from the first moment we met, but I don't see him hiring a killer or anyone who will shoot you in the kneecaps."

"You don't understand. He can make people get sick from a distance, just like he made Nadia walk over hot coals. You've heard it yourself with your own ears."

"True, but I never saw it myself with my own eyes. Listen, you keep saying the words 'do you see' and 'do you get it' as though I couldn't grasp the idea. But instead it's you who doesn't understand that you are dealing with a professional swindler. Francesca, wake up and take advantage of the fact that I came looking for you and that I am here."

"Yes, thank you, but I know that you cannot understand" Francesca said. ("Here we go again …" thought Elena.) "He's told me this and he's threatened to do this to me as well as to my family … even if he did take it back later. We were arguing and it slipped out of his mouth without his wanting to, then he apologized and laughed about it, but I'm afraid of him. He has strange powers … he knows how the human mind works and above all he knows how very receptive my mind is. You see, we are two poles that are attracted to each other for good as well as for bad, so I shouldn't provoke him, but only love him…"

"And obviously he told you this as well…" said Elena, seeing very clearly that it was not a slight case of domination but more like reducing someone to mental slavery. She was beginning to get desperate about being able to convince Francesca. After all, Elena was not a professional therapist, that is, someone who could really help Francesca to escape from the claws of that criminal.

But she wanted to try once more, so she said "Francesca, that's enough now, really. You have to shake your brain out of that passive torpor that Marco has wrapped you in. Stop saying such silly things."

"He's even taken out some of the money from our joint bank account where I deposited it. You know, last month I received my part of the inheritance that Massimo and I were counting on to put things back into place and to buy ourselves a nice sailboat. How will I manage anywhere else?"

"Oh, now you are talking like a rational human being and about the concrete problems he has given you. What a clever rascal! And now we can see the whole picture."

"Don't say that. It's just another strategy for keeping me beside him. He can't live without me."

Elena did not in the least consider replying to this last enormous piece of nonsense pronounced by Francesca, and limited herself to adding, "I've already told you that you are coming to me. Instead, are you sure that you've nothing more to tell me about this scoundrel? What did you call him — the Charmer? Where is your pride, Francesca? Tomorrow let's go together to see my lawyer friend, Manfredi."

It was raining cats and dogs the next day while they were driving to the appointment with Manfredi. Elena had contacted him right away, and he had just as quickly made himself available.

"Elena, what a pleasure! It must be something important if you've called me at the office. No, don't worry, a client has just left and the next one won't be here for another quarter of an hour. Tell me briefly what it is all about."

"Well, look, it's not directly for me, but I would be really grateful if you could see my cousin and me as soon as possible."

"You sound quite worried. Just give me an idea of what kind of problem Francesca has. I remember her perfectly — who could not? I know that she separated from her husband because one of my colleagues handled it. What's going on now?"

"What's happened is that she left one guy and ended up with an even worse one. There's a lot of money involved that needs to be recovered."

"Let me check my agenda ... come tomorrow afternoon — late afternoon — the both of you. I'll tell my secretary to squeeze you in between one client and another. Ciao. See you tomorrow."

While they were in the car on the following afternoon, Elena had decided to get Francesca to come out with everything else that still remained to be said about the case because she was afraid that Francesca might not mention things in front of Manfredi, either in defense of Marco or because she was afraid of him.

"I don't know how the hell you ever managed to stay in that relationship without going crazy" she said (stopping herself in time so as not to say "unless we admit that you are crazy already").

"I used to wake up at night and I would start meditating, the way that he taught us in our group sessions. You don't how much that can help suffering souls…"

("Here we go again" Elena thought.) But she said only "I see. What did you meditate on in the middle of the night?"

"Oh, you don't always meditate on the same things, it depends on the situation and on what you need when life puts things in your path…"

"So…"

"…about the transcendent communion of thoughts and affection that binds people together — like Marco and me, for example — or about how unimportant are possessions and material things — including the body, which too often demands sex as a means of communication. Then I would drift back to sleep. And the next day was another day…"

("And so that's why you have shrunk down to a skeleton and you are penniless — because material things are not important," Elena silently told herself. "He jets back and forth while earning a shitload of money with his profession and you are stupid enough to give him yours as well.")

They arrived at Manfredi's office after about three-quarters of an hour and the secretary informed him of their arrival over the intercom.

After the conventional ritual of shaking hands and the how-long-has-it-beens, Francesca laid out the case, and Manfredi could not help but note the apologetic tone which she used when referring to the absent man, as though she felt that she was at fault for the accusations which Elena was forcing her to make.

Elena and Manfredi exchanged a meaningful glance and Manfredi at once understood the problem, even though she had not been able to give him any details at all of the history, because she had called him from the breakfast table during a brief break when Francesca had gone to answer the telephone.

It was the usual swindle by the live-in partner: with the excuse of helping to save on the banking charges, one partner offered to safeguard the other's money by putting it into his own bank account.

Manfredi made it clear from the start that the probabilities of a successful swindle were directly proportionate to how much the other person was enamored. But the odds of winning the case also depended on the same variable, because he would have to dig into the history of their relationship with lucid cruelty.

Elena understood that her friend was choosing his words very carefully so as not to offend Francesca. He had used the euphemism 'enamored' so as not to speak of stupidity and gullibility.

He asked Francesca if she had decided to proceed in the recovery of her money and added, "Perhaps you should now tell me the name of this gentleman."

"Yes, of course ... but I'm not sure yet. Perhaps I should have thought about it for a while longer before coming here to take up your time. As for the name of my common-law-husband, he is Doctor Marco Rossi, the psychiatrist."

A few seconds of heavy silence passed, during which Elena asked herself what the reason could be, and then she asked "Excuse me, Manfredi, but what's wrong?"

"Because your cousin had just named the biggest delinquent I know. So far, we've never managed to nail him down because he has strong connections and because his threats have already forced two women to renounce bringing charges against him."

"What do you mean?" asked Francesca, as she tried to maintain a respectful tone.

"I'm saying that this lovely little package… First of all, he is not a psychiatrist. Second, he has played the same little game with you that he did before with another two poor women like you. And all of this more or less within the last ten years. He keeps a low profile. Usually he gets whichever companion he has at the time to put her name on the rental contracts for his villas and he holes up there like a mole in his hiding place. Not only is he not listed anywhere as a professional, but he has already received two official complaints from the Board of Psychiatrists. Plus, the complaints which were taken back after he made threats against the two women who used to be his companions. Is that enough for you, Elena, or should I go on?"

"That's more than enough for me," answered Elena, understanding perfectly that Manfredi had begun to doubt Francesca's sanity.

It was also enough for Francesca. After the shock inflicted by Elena's friend, she now felt ashamed to find herself declassed — demoted to being the moll of a petty criminal and not the common-law wife of the great luminary in whom she had believed.

That was exactly what her mind — deceived, but still proud — deserved, even if that pride was only due to the light reflected off her partner. She barely spoke the whole way home.

"Are you processing the information?" chanced Elena, though it was clear that Francesca was processing something else entirely. It was the downfall of two myths: one personified by Marco and the other one by herself. Elena left her to her own thoughts and, that evening, she prepared their dinner.

The next morning, when they met in the kitchen, Francesca hugged Elena and said in a whisper "Thank you. What would I have done if you had not come to find me? My bags are packed. I'll leave the keys with his sister."

"Good for you. This is what I like to see. Don't worry, we'll fix everything. Manfredi is smart and he'll make him pay, you'll see. Especially now that he's so riled up and looking for justice. The Scarlet Pimpernel may have struck again but this time much too close to him. You are my cousin, and Manfredi and I are really good friends."

"But how will I pay him?"

"Don't worry. Between the two of us, we'll help you. You can count on it. And, anyway, you'll have your money back within a few months, right?"

"You've been so present in my life, without being intrusive, but luckily you finally took the situation in hand. Thank you for getting me out of Hell."

It would sound like a story with a happy ending, but for the fact that it hasn't ended yet.

For the next two years, Francesca and Elena continued to see each other. Elena had realized quite early on that Francesca would need help to demolish the mental superstructure that Marco had superimposed on her mental faculties. It would take time; she had known that from the very beginning. So she patiently absorbed Francesca's recurrent lucubration on how much she missed the group-therapy sessions that she had presided over and on how a sudden pain in her shoulder was surely caused by 'Him' (because by now Marco no longer existed for Francesca, who could never admit to herself that she had been involved with a mere commoner).

She often repeated the same questions to Elena: How could he have pretended with everyone to be a psychiatrist? How could he have dared to practice such a refined profession and get away with it so well ... without even a degree...? Evidently she was getting there bit by bit. Soon she would be free — her mind free — from that shadow which darkened all her thoughts.

There were times though, when Elena could not stand it anymore and she would have loved to have said that it wasn't only 'Him' but also 'Her' who had practiced without a license — even though she was the injured party and even though she had only had a small part in it. Francesca had also shared that (to use her own words) 'refined profession' in which what was put at risk was the minds of the patients.

But Elena never said any of that as she waited for Francesca to get stronger and to accept herself without any trace of that cultural superiority which Marco had convinced her that she possessed.

As the months passed, Elena believed that she saw her cousin get her feet back on the ground.

"I think that I should take the first job I can get, even as a caregiver," Francesca said one day, sometime after she had 'escaped' from the gilded cage of her relationship.

"Don't put it that way," Elena consoled her, even though she had eagerly waited for some similar home truth to come from those lips. "Think about it in terms of being a lady's companion. Maybe we will manage to find an elderly lady who needs someone to read aloud to her for a few hours and some pleasant conversation."

"Oh, how sad. Anyway, I need to do something even if I can finally leave your house and not have to worry about rent, since my brother is going to give me the other half of his duplex house for a few years."

"You see? Slowly but surely, your family as well is welcoming you back. Of course, they couldn't forgive so easily the money that you naively let Marco steal from you, but knowing that Manfredi is getting it back makes them less upset. We did the right thing in telling them about it."

"I know. And when I think that it might have helped to keep the ship of my marriage afloat..." and then Francesca had looked at Elena and burst into gales of laughter. It had been the first real laugh — straight from the heart — since those days when, like a trained seal, she only smiled or laughed at Marco's command. And she had continued "The symbolic ship, that is. The one that the rats abandon when it is about to sink. That's what my ex-husband used to say about me when he referred to me and him. For sure, the money would have been better spent if we had bought his dreamboat — the real one, I mean." And then she had smiled again.

"Could it be that she's getting a little bit of a sense of humor after all these setbacks?" thought Elena.

"I ran off with Marco all of a sudden, just when I was about to get that money which for years Massimo and I had been waiting for. The Charmer knew perfectly well that the money was about to come to me."

"A good thing that you yourself arrived at the fact. That move must have seemed so dirty to Massimo, don't you think? Never mind, it's all water under the bridge now. Tell me instead how things are going with your sisters."

"They are doing their utmost to help. They even pass some money over to me to buy new clothes. You are so right, we are becoming a family again. Or it might be better to say that they are including me in the family again because they were never divided and were totally in agreement in accusing me of behaving badly in the way I left Massimo. They were right, too. I'd even add that they never criticized the end of the marriage itself".

"I'm glad for you. Now you can concentrate exclusively on finding a job."

Elena could never have foreseen that her newly embraced family, by making her life easier, had done none other than reawaken in her malleable mind the pride of the Privileged Few.

Within a month Francesca's talk was the exact opposite of when she had even been willing to become a caregiver.

"I can't accept work which is beneath me" she was heard to brusquely declare one day.

"What do you mean?" Elena pressed.

"I mean to say that we are not all equal. We aren't and that's just how it is — either by birth or by stroke of luck or by whatever you think it is. And if someone wants me, they will have to offer me something commensurate with my level. I can even do without an extra pair of boots until that point."

Elena caught the gist immediately. Now (thanks to the intervention of her siblings) that the real worries had been resolved (a roof over her head and how to meet daily expenses), Francesca had regressed to the state of spoiled little girl, just as she had always lived.

"But have you ever considered that in some circumstances an extra pair of boots constitutes an item of luxury and not a basic need? Don't you think that what you need above all else is to earn your own income? Won't you need this for food and to meet all those expenses which you are sure to incur?"

"As far as that goes and by good fortune, you know that my family is helping me out. I have a roof over my head. I'll wait for someone to offer me a consultancy or whatever."

("Here we go again," thought Elena, "more omnipotent ravings...") But she limited her question to "Right, and what kind of 'whatever' would that be?"

"What can I tell you right now? Any position would be fine with me, as long as it matches my competencies. Nothing more, but certainly nothing less. After all, you know that I have a deep knowledge of psychology and design and fashion... As long as my terms are met, I'll take the first job that comes along."

"And just how are these consultancies supposed to come along? As far as I know, you are not enrolled on any professional Register."

"Oh, the channels are many and multiform... I'll craft my curriculum vitae ("with what diplomas?" thought Elena). and I'll send it around to the big fashion houses and to the best stylists. I've already started to contact my professional friends who used to be in the same circle as Massimo and me."

"But have you weighed the fact that you left scorched earth behind you when you left Massimo the way that you did? Renato told me that all your friends were on his side then."

"Elena, don't force me to say things that only apparently will sound arrogant, especially because you are not ugly either, but as soon as I pick up the phone and let people know that I'm still alive, then no one will be able to resist the desire to see me again. Especially given that I am single again."

All that good humility of the previous months was no more than the product of her cousin's short-lived fear at finding herself alone. That is, without a gallant knight willing to slay all the dragons on the Earth in order to win her. And fear from not yet finding herself back in the bosom of her elitist family.

Even without her two Pygmalions, Francesca had by now regained a notable dose of self-esteem — not to say arrogance — which had been covered only momentarily by the ashes of adversity. For that matter, ever since she was a girl, she had possessed a sense of worth, even before her two major tutors had taught her to lose her natural shyness, stemming from not having yet experimented with her natural endowments.

Every day that passed made her stronger and more able to walk on her own two feet, even if she was only walking around in circles, wasting time, which Elena never tired of giving her advice on how to fill. Say, with a course of study that would furnish her with a certificate with which to find a job.

She spent her days getting ready to go out and reading those glossy magazines that she could never entirely give up. They were the same magazines that had driven her husband crazy during the last part of their marriage, when she would come home with only half the food shopping but with the latest black-lacquered issue of her favorite art magazine or the latest issue of Vogue under her arm.

While this metamorphosis was taking place inside her, she moved into the house which her brother had put at her disposition. It was completely furnished and in that good taste which everyone in her family seemed to have, but Francesca managed to give it her personal touch as well, and the result was superb.

Immediately afterwards — perhaps it had been no more than a week — the visits to Elena's house began to diminish and Elena began to receive fewer calls from her. The excuses offered for this change were due to her being busy with things that were never defined in terms that ordinary people used.

Francesca would say that she had dropped by the city center to study the shop window of a famous stylist in order to get some ideas. Or she would have gone to a book store to look for a book on experimental auto-analysis, because she had left her copy behind with Marco — left, that is, in the sense that it belonged to him and she had consulted it or maybe even read the whole thing when she was preparing for the group therapy sessions. In fact, starting up a self-help group that she could direct had rather caught her fancy.

Elena asked herself where the money was coming from, until one day when Francesca said to her with great simplicity that she had got in touch again with that friend of hers, the Head Physician, with whom she had been having an affair but broke it off when she suddenly left home for Marco.

When Francesca had told her this bit of history, Elena had asked herself "What about Massimo?" Francesca had not even mentioned him and Elena had no information about what had happened during that ten-year gap when they had stopped seeing each other. But she let the story emerge spontaneously from the lips of the party concerned, without asking a single question, so as not to risk Francesca stopping the tale in a kind of self-censure. This would, of course, pre-suppose that Francesca had a conscience. And Francesca did not.

"You know, he couldn't have asked for anything more. Imagine — he waited for me for all these years. He was crazy about me then and he still is. It's just that before we were in the same boat because we were both married. But now everything is different and I'm the one leading the game."

"What do you mean?"

"Just that I like him a lot — just as much as before — but if he was so crazy as to forgive me for leaving him from one day to the next for another man … well, he knows that I could run away again, doesn't he? And especially now that I am single and completely free. Like you, and you don't have to give an account of yourself to anyone either, do you?"

("As if you ever gave a fig about treating your husband honestly in that marriage," Elena silently commented to herself.)

So that's where the money was coming from. It wasn't a

lot, but it was what a married man — with a profession and well-to-do — could detract from the family budget without anyone noticing.

Elena did not know what to say and was quiet for a few seconds. Then Francesca, feeling that her morality was being judged, added in an arrogant tone "Do I have to repeat that I don't owe anyone an explanation … and I do not intend to even consider what you think."

Evidently she knew her best friend well and she knew perfectly well that Elena did not agree with her behavior regarding the fact that whenever her friend the Doctor stayed with her, that he would leave some money on the table or on the bedside table and that Francesca would accept it.

"He can't be going into the shops to buy me presents … after all, it's the same thing."

Egocentric and lacking any inhibitions — when it had to do with her own self-interest, Francesca thought that it was all quite natural, that it was normal behavior.

Elena again found before her that haughty girl who she had always known, the one who had ensnared Massimo, but who now lacked the timidity that had once come out now and again.

Forever concerned only with herself, Francesca began to come out with strange comments:

"Of course, you work hard, Elena — Monday, Tuesday, Wednesday, etcetera. But when do you ever enjoy yourself?" or "How is it possible that you can never go with me to the Outlets except on Sundays? On Sundays, I have other things that I want to do."

Until the day arrived when, even though for two weeks beforehand they had been planning to go to see an exhibition together, Elena heard her say, "Look, I want to go by myself and I want to go whenever I feel like it. I don't want ties of any kind now that I am completely free — and also free from being afraid of Marco, even at a distance." She had hesitated for a few seconds and then she exploded with "And I don't want to hear you say that you helped me to get out of his house, because I did it on my own two legs!"

Elena, who had not even thought about claiming any merit for herself, reflected in that moment on how it was all true. But outside, waiting in the car, had been Elena and God only knows if Francesca could ever have done it by herself.